Richard Leary—scientist, educator, historian. Leary earned a B.S. at Virginia Tech, an M.S. at the University of Michigan, and a Ph.D. at the University of Illinois; all in geology. In graduate school he minored in the classics. His interest in history has expanded since, from ancient Greece, pre-Roman Italy (the Etruscans) and early Christianity to the history of Lake Ann, Michigan, where he and his wife, Eleanor, spend their summers.

Richard was curator of geology at the Illinois State Museum for over thirty-five years. In addition to writing scientific papers, he published many articles in the *Living Museum*, the newsletter of the Illinois State Museum. He also published articles on local history in the *Grand Traverse Journal*, the online journal of Traverse City, Michigan.

Leary is an active Presbyterian church member in Springfield, Illinois. The many educational programs there inspired his interest in Christian history and Mary Magdalene.

This story is fiction, in particular, historical fiction. It is heavily influenced by the author's imagination. But, that said, it is based on ancient texts, including the New Testament, and ancient traditions. Most of the people in this story were real people, who lived 2,000 years ago. They participated in some of the events described in these pages.

But this is a fictionalized version of the people, places and events.

The portrayal of all characters and events in this novel is the product of the author's fertile imagination. Although inspired by many people and literary works, this interpretation of the past is the author's own creation.

Mary Magdalene

A Woman with a Mission

Richard Leary

Mary Magdalene

A Woman with a Mission

Vanguard Press

VANGUARD PAPERBACK

© Copyright 2024
Richard Leary

The right of Richard Leary to be identified as author of
this work has been asserted by him in accordance with the
Copyright, Designs and Patents Act 1988.

All Rights Reserved

No reproduction, copy or transmission of this publication
may be made without written permission.
No paragraph of this publication may be reproduced,
copied or transmitted save with the written permission of the
publisher, or in accordance with the provisions
of the Copyright Act 1956 (as amended).

Any person who commits any unauthorised act in relation to
this publication may be liable to criminal
prosecution and civil claims for damages.

A CIP catalogue record for this title is
available from the British Library.

ISBN 978-1-80016-567-0

Vanguard Press is an imprint of
Pegasus Elliot Mackenzie Publishers Ltd.
www.pegasuspublishers.com

First Published in 2024

Vanguard Press
Sheraton House Castle Park
Cambridge England

Printed & Bound in Great Britain

Acknowledgements

Thanks to all who have, over the past several years, listened to my ruminations on this topic. Most have done so willingly, and I really appreciate their support and comments. I especially appreciate those who read early renditions of the manuscript as it has grown from an essay to a short story to a novella.

I would like to give special thanks to some friends who provided special assistance. These include Charles Schweighauser, Carole and Jay Kennerly and Gary Vitale who corrected grammar and spelling, made suggestions on content, and offered encouragement. But despite their best efforts, this is my writing; I am responsible for the text and any errors or offenses.

I especially want to thank my wife, Eleanor, for listening to my frequent rambling about obscure events and offering suggestions. I appreciate her proof reading of several versions of this multiyear work. She proved to have a real knack for spotting errors.

I should also thank my wife for her understanding of the 'other woman in my life' with whom I spent many hours and evenings.

I should not omit the many people who taught short courses or gave lectures that educated me and inspired me to dig deeper into history. There are too many to name because they came into my life from childhood Sunday school teachers to present day pastors and class leaders.

I encourage readers, especially younger readers, to search out and take advantage of educational opportunities. The more you know, the richer your life will be. The broader your knowledge, the better person you will be, the better prepared you will be to understand people you will meet in life.

Contents

Author's Note 13
Prologue 17
Map showing locations of cities mentioned in text ... 23
Chapter One
Maria's Mission 25
Chapter Two
Growing up in Magdala 42
Chapter Three
A Messiah Emerges 62
Chapter Four
Maria and Her Friends Join Jesus 77
Chapter Five
Maria Begins her Mission 100
Chapter Six
The Emergence of Paul 126
Chapter Seven
Disagreement Among the Disciples 132
Chapter Eight
Maria's 'Mission Journey' 143
Map showing cities Mary Magdalene visited
on her way from Galilee to Gaul. 151
Chapter Nine
The 'Mission Trip' Becomes a True Missionary
Journey 152
Chapter Ten
The Long Journey Continues 166
Chapter Eleven
The Crucifixion and Conclusion 182
Epilogue 197
APPENDIX 201

Author's Note

Although this is a fictionalized biography of Mary Magdalene, I have endeavored to make it as accurate as possible. Perhaps rather than saying the story is 'accurate', it is more honest to say it is 'consistent with' what we know from limited, incomplete and inconsistent sources. It is based on the New Testament gospels, several non-canonical texts that mention Mary Magdalene and French traditions of her later life in southern France.

Although the traditions of Mary Magdalene in France may be just traditions, they make a good story and provide a unique way to tell her story. I have also based parts of the story on my knowledge, as a non-professional, of first century life in Galilee and southern Gaul.

The New Testament gospels are often inconsistent and, having been written decades after the events they describe, may not be completely accurate. The non-canonical texts, written even later and with particular biases and points of view, may not reflect actual events.

The French traditions about Mary Magdalene date back at least to the 800s. They were widespread in the Middle Ages and were the result of a desire to bring pilgrims to particular churches and towns. They brought status to a church as well as donations. Pilgrims also brought income to merchants and providers of food and lodging in cities on pilgrimage routes.

It is, however, possible that these French traditions, like some Greek and Roman legends, may have a kernel of truth behind them. For example, the story of Jason and the Golden Fleece may reflect the use of sheep's fleece to catch fine gold particles in slice boxes where gold-bearing sediment was processed.

With these caveats in mind, I have tried to present a realistic account of Mary Magdalene's life.

Regardless, the truth is that Mary Magdalene played a major role in the spread of the story and message of Jesus and the development of early Christianity. The non-canonical gospels, many found buried in Egypt, prove that Mary Magdalene had many followers and was held in high regard over a vast region of the Middle East at least as late as the fourth century.

The creators of the original 'universal' or 'Catholic' church in the third and fourth centuries strove to diminish the role of women during the life of Jesus and immediately following the resurrection.

They made keeping women out of the church hierarchy a priority. Had they not been so androcentric, Mary Magdalene would be honored along with Peter and Paul as a founder of the faith.

Although denied a prominent place in the Western Church, Mary Magdalene does have a place of honor in the Eastern Orthodox Church.

I hope this account will restore her story to history.

The Names Mary and Maria

In the West, we know the subject of this story as Mary Magdalene. In the ancient world she was known as Maria (or Miriam). In the Greek of the New Testament (e.g. Matthew 27:56), she was Μαρια η Μαγδαληνη (Mary the Magdalene). In order to reflect that ancient period, the time when she lived, I have chosen to use 'Maria'.

Prologue

The battle against the heretics.

The warmth of the midsummer sun brought forth good crops in the lush agricultural land along the Mediterranean shore of southern France. Farmers, working the productive soil, enjoyed a slack season between the intensive labors of planting and harvest.

Like most people in their communities, they had little contact with or knowledge of the world beyond their borders. However, this year, travelers and merchants brought with them rumors from far away, telling the people living in the vicinity of Beziers that the papal army was approaching. Some of the local Catholics, knowing that the church had labeled them 'heretics', began to withdraw behind the city walls. Soon, other Catholics, uncertain of what might happen when the army arrived, began gathering within the city walls as well.

Beziers was a large city, almost 30,000 strong, with a large cathedral and castle, surrounded by stout walls. Located twenty-five miles from the Mediterranean coast and 110 miles west of Marseille,

France, it was a little farther west of St. Maximin, the center of Mary Magdalene's preaching. By the twelfth century, it was clearly within the region affected by the Christian message espoused by Mary Magdalene centuries earlier.

In early July of 1209, the pope's army, augmented by several hundred mercenaries, reached Beziers. The Cistercian abbot, Arraud Amairy, who led the army, only wanted to punish those who refused to accept fully all the teachings and leadership of the church in Rome.

When the army arrived, they found the city gates closed and the countryside virtually empty of its inhabitants. The massive army surrounded the city. With the large number of armed troops, weapons glittering in the sun, and the presence of huge machines of war, their intentions were clear.

The abbot demanded entry into the city but was rebuffed. The city leaders, as well as the general population, had heard what the troops, under orders from Rome, had done to others labeled 'heretics' by the church leaders in Rome. The people of Beziers hoped they could convince the generals of the besieging army that they were faithful and obedient Catholics. Failing that, they hoped their stout city walls would keep out the pope's army.

The so-called 'heretics' were attacked by the pope's army because they, like the Eastern Orthodox

Church, believed in local leadership and a limited hierarchy. They resisted the central and distant control in the person of the pope. These dissidents also allowed women to participate on an equal basis with men in their ministry, as Jesus and the Apostle Paul had done.

However, it was the rejection of the pope that sent the church in Rome into a rage. It was not just the Cathars in France that believed that the office of pope was contrary to the teachings of Jesus. Christians in the Eastern Orthodox Church did not recognize the office of pope; nor did those Christians in Egypt and Ethiopia.

Clearly the officials in Rome had to stop the spread of this dissent. The city of Beziers in southern France was a good place to begin due to its size and prominence. The city was not protected by an organized military, but by poorly armed local men, mostly farmers. They were no match for the large, well-armed and well-trained soldiers sent by Rome.

When the leaders of the army and the mercenaries asked the abbot how they were to separate the heretics from the good Catholics, the abbot simply said, "Kill them all. The Lord knows his own." When the men seemed alarmed, he shrugged and said that was the word from Rome.

Battering rams were brought to the main city gate. Catapults hurled huge stones at the massive city walls. Those people inside the city fought valiantly. For several days they shot arrows down from the ramparts, keeping the attacking army and its machines of war from getting close to the walls. They hurled large stones down on the attackers, taking a heavy toll.

Eventually the people within the city walls exhausted their supply of missiles and stones used against the attacking army. The gates were smashed, and the walls breached. The soldiers systematically moved through the city, putting to the sword every person they encountered. Men, women, and children were cut down. Old men and women in their beds were hacked to death. People were pulled from hiding places and put to death.

The soldiers went through the city methodically, block by block, house by house. Every out building was thoroughly searched. No cabinet, cupboard or pantry went unopened.

The cathedral stood on high ground near the center of the city. It was a large and imposing Romanesque structure, located on a central square. The massive stone building was designed to impress and inspire visitors to the city and residents as well. In this it certainly succeeded.

The interior was spacious and open, built to hold large numbers of worshippers. The decoration was not ornate. The few statues of saints were there to educate, not to attract a wandering eye during the services. As the army surged through the city, many more of the faithful took refuge in the high church, crowding into its huge sanctuary. They hoped their devotion would save them, in the next world if not in this one. Priests put on their vestments and ordered the church bells to ring. They said a mass for the dead, and for themselves.

Soldiers set the church on fire and killed anyone who tried to escape. Several thousand died in the church that day.

The army continued into the heart of the city, intent on pillaging the castle. The massive castle, built centuries earlier to defend the local rulers, stood at the highest point in the city. Many people rushed within its thick walls seeking protection. But even there the invaders broke in and killed all those inside. The castle was pillaged, looted, and burned.

When the invaders reached the far side of the city, they started back toward the main gate, setting fires as they went. Every building, storage shed, wagon and haystack, anything that would burn, was set ablaze.

When the soldiers again came to the main gate through which they had entered, they looked back to see devastation and death, growing flames and billowing smoke.

As the city lay devastated and smoke rose from the ruins, two mercenaries sat outside the city walls. Their faces were smudged with soot and dirt. Their clothes soaked with sweat and splotched with blood. They were too exhausted to walk farther without a rest.

One of the men, after a long silence, queried the other, "What exactly did these people believe that so offended the church in Rome? How could a difference in theology justify such slaughter?"

The answer was complicated, but the origin of the heresy went back centuries, to the first Christian converts in Gaul. It went back to the teachings of Jesus, Paul and a few other early apostles, teachings brought to Gaul by Mary Magdalene.

The root of the problem was Mary Magdalene herself. She came to Gaul soon after the death and resurrection of Christ, preaching the gospel and winning many converts. Mary Magdalene, whom the church in Rome labeled a prostitute, had brought this 'heresy' to the region. As a result, the French heretics had a special relationship with Mary Magdalene, one of Jesus' most devoted followers.

Even if it required centuries, the church would stamp out her memory and her heritage. Or so the church hoped.

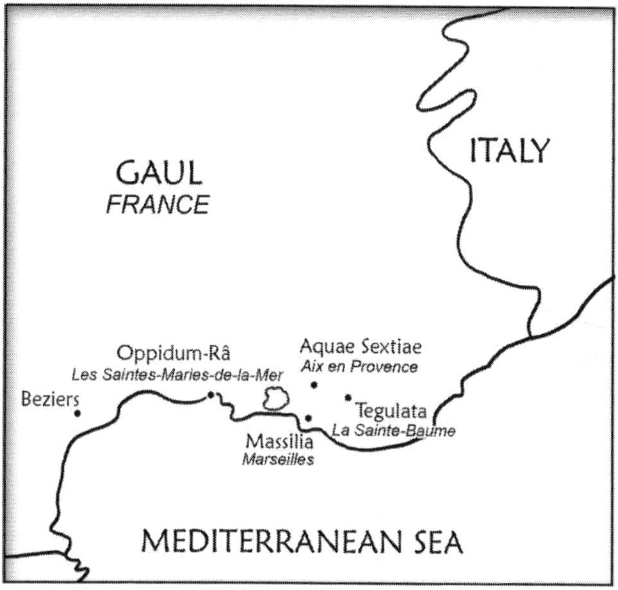

Map showing locations of cities mentioned in text

Chapter One

Maria's Mission

The Gospel in Gaul

Marcus had so many questions: Why had Maria Magdalene decided to come here, to Gaul, so far from home and family? How did she get here? He was eager to meet this impressive woman, a follower, no, not just a follower, but a companion of Jesus. He was anxious to meet Maria and hear the answers to his questions directly from her. The anticipation drove Marcus to quicken his steps.

The sun was just coming up on a beautiful autumn day, brisk but with the promise of becoming warm and sunny. The trees were in full, glorious color. Marcus, a young Roman, walked along a narrow but well-worn path that paralleled a small stream. The path lay between the stream and the base of a steep cliff composed of thick layers of gray and tan rock.

Over many millennia, seeping groundwater had eroded caves deep within the limestone exposed near the path. Now the openings were unseen, hidden behind thick bushes and trees. In winter, once the leaves had fallen, and in spring, before branches were again covered in leaves, the dark, often mysterious, entrances to caves were visible.

It was early October in southern Gaul, a Roman province in southern France.[1] It had been a Roman province since 121 B.C. and the Roman presence was widespread. Some former soldiers had received plots of land here when they retired from the Roman military. In addition to the influence of the Roman military, many Roman civilians had settled there as well. It was 54 A.D., and the emperor Claudius ruled the Roman Empire.

Marcus, like most Romans, had been a pagan. He lived in a world of many gods and goddesses — such as Jupiter, Venus, and Mars — as well as family spirits known as *gens*. His family had a small shrine for them on one wall where they lit candles or burned incense on special days.

Marcus had not been a strong believer in the various gods and goddesses, nor was he involved in their worship. Nevertheless, they were always in the background, their temples always present and prominent. These deities were believed to affect the lives of citizens and the fate of the empire.

---

[1] As everyone who took Latin in high school remembers the words of Caesar, *"Omnia Gallia in tres partes divisa est."* (All Gaul is divided into three parts.)

Roman authorities made them impossible to ignore because public sacrifices were obligatory. Roman citizens were also required to worship the emperor and make public offerings to him as well. Failure to do so brought serious punishment, even death.

Living in a remote area such as southern Gaul made it easy to avoid the religious festivals and offerings ordered by government officials. Such circumstances made it easy for Marcus to leave the Roman gods and join the Way.

Marcus came to Gaul from central Italy with the Roman army several years earlier. He had been stationed in Aquae Sextiae[2], a Roman city founded in 123 B.C. by the Roman consul Sextius Calvinus. The city was situated near several prominent springs, hence the name Aquae Sextiae, *aquae* being the Latin word for water. Marcus served in a Roman garrison established to maintain peace and protect Roman settlers and merchants.

Impressed by the beauty of the region and fertility of the land, Marcus remained after his military service ended. He sought available land outside the large city in order to plant a vineyard. He had made a home in Tegulata[3], a city surrounded by rich farm land. Tegulata was east of Aquae Sextiae but close enough

---

[2] The city is now known as Aix-en-Provence.
[3] Now named La Sainte-Baume.

to the port of Massilia[4] for access to the Mediterranean Sea.

Marcus was in his early thirties, tall (by first century standards), ruggedly handsome with dark hair and eyes. His body was muscular from lifting heavy terracotta amphoras of wine. He was confident, had a pleasant nature and the ability to communicate and to persuade people. These attributes made him a successful businessman. They also helped him make friends among the local people and he enjoyed joining them for meals and festivals.

As an officer in the Roman army Marcus was knowledgeable about history, geography, engineering, natural history, and forces of nature such as wind and currents in the Mediterranean. All this knowledge benefitted him as he established himself in southern Gaul.

Centuries earlier, the residents of Narbonensis, as the southern province of Gaul was known, imported wine from Etruria, the Italian region north of Rome. The Gauls later learned from the Etruscans how to make wine and brought grape vines to Gaul. The plants did well on the rocky slopes unsuited for growing wheat and other crops. Many vineyards were planted, and wine production increased over the following decades. Now, by the first century A.D. wines from Gaul were in demand throughout the Roman Empire.

---

[4] Now Marseilles.

In the army Marcus developed organizational skills that greatly helped him in creating vineyards, a winery and selling his products over a large area. His contacts with fellow soldiers, now scattered in the empire, and current members of the army also helped him develop markets for his wines.

He earned a good living buying quantities of wine — measured in hundreds of clay amphoras, each holding about twenty-six liters — from producers in the region around Tegulata. He hauled the loads of wine to Massilia and sold it to merchants who exported it to distant Mediterranean ports in Italy and North Africa. He also had a small winery himself with several hectares of grape vines. Young Marcus was clearly a successful businessman but, despite his success and good looks, he was still unmarried.

Now, Marcus was pleased to have an excuse to leave the city and enjoy a walk in the countryside. The path he walked was lined with tall trees, overarching the path. He noted the evergreen pines and the oaks whose leaves still clung to the branches. Large leaves from the *platanes,* a relative of the sycamore tree, were already falling and collecting along the path. During the hot summer months these trees offered welcome shade from the intense Mediterranean sun.

Marcus always had an interest in and curiosity about the world around him. As he ascended into the hills he thought about the history of the small valley.

He wondered how it was before people came to the region.

The path between the stream and cliff had existed for centuries, no doubt begun by animals moving along the valley. Over the years, people had cut rough steps into the bedrock at steep slopes along the path. They had also arranged stepping stones across small streams flowing from springs at the base of the cliff.

Marcus had been sent by Jeanne, a friend of many years, to meet Maria, the woman who brought the teachings of Jesus Christ to the region. It was Maria who had converted Jeanne and her family to Christianity several years earlier, becoming a close friend as well. Jeanne wanted to share this message of salvation with Marcus because it had made such an impression on her and so changed her family's life. Jeanne liked Marcus very much and felt strongly that she needed to bring Marcus and Maria together.

Maria had converted many people in the region, both Gauls and Romans, to Christianity. The natives of Gaul were pagans who worshipped various aspects of nature. Romans had brought a variety of pagan gods and goddesses to the area from many parts of the Roman Empire. Each group had offered its own challenges to Maria's efforts to convert them to monotheism and bring them into the fellowship of Jesus and the Way.

Maria came to southern Gaul from Israel many years earlier, a story unto itself. As she became acquainted with local residents, she talked of her earlier life and told of her experiences with Jesus, the Messiah. After years of preaching about the Way and warning of the coming judgment and kingdom of God, she retreated to a small cave near the Roman city of Tegulata. It was to this cave that Jeanne had given directions to Marcus, together with a letter of introduction.

The morning was brisk and invigorating. Near the city the air carried the smell of smoke as people lit fires to warm their cottages after the chill of the autumn night and began to prepare breakfast.

As Marcus walked along the path, he breathed deeply from the brisk, fresh morning air. He thought of the woman he was going to see. His friend Jeanne had often spoken of this fascinating woman who now lived alone in a cave an hour's walk outside the city. Jeanne had talked of her intelligence and her remarkable life before coming to southern Gaul.

Marcus had heard about Maria not only from Jeanne but also from workers in his vineyard, men who worked his grape presses, and the wine makers. Each worker seemed to have his own favorite story about Maria.

As he thought of all he had heard about her, he walked a little faster, eager to meet her and to hear these stories directly from her. From what he had already heard, he knew there were many amazing parts in Maria's life experiences. He had many questions to ask her.

Marcus came to a large boulder near the path, a landmark that Jeanne had included in her directions. At this point a hardly discernible path angled up the slope toward the cliff. Marcus followed the path through the bushes covered with yellow and crimson leaves. The dew on the leaves soaked his tunic, adding to the chill of the morning.

As he approached the mouth of the cave, he called out, "Maria, Maria." Hearing no answer, he continued until he reached the low, wide opening.

The cave entrance was at the back of a large overhang in the cliff, appearing as a dark shadow in the light-colored stone. The cave itself was at ground level and more than head high. It appeared to extend some distance into the mountain, but the darkness prevented him from discerning the actual depth.

Again he called out, "Maria, Maria."

This time a woman's voice responded, "Yes, who calls? Come over here."

A slender woman emerged from the shadows of the cave entrance. She was of moderate height but stood erect. She walked gracefully over the uneven ground as she moved toward Marcus. Her face expressed a warm welcome, putting Marcus at ease.

Maria was modestly dressed in a simple flax tunic and outer woolen cloak. She wore a woolen shawl over her shoulders in the cool mornings and evenings. Her hair was gray and, when not tied up with a strip of cloth, hung to just below her shoulders. Her complexion was lighter than it was when she arrived in Gaul from the eastern end of the Mediterranean Sea years earlier. Despite her advanced age — she was now in her fifties — her skin was smooth and unblemished.

Maria knew all too well of the persecution of Christians by Rome and so she felt some apprehension when she saw a Roman approaching. However, Marcus' pleasant appearance made her relax. She even sensed some apprehension in his expression.

Maria was happy to have a visitor because not as many people came to see her as when she first moved here from the city. She was actually glad to have a young Roman. She thought, *He will talk to his friends and help spread the message of Jesus and the Way.* She also wondered what he wanted and who had encouraged him to come.

Marcus introduced himself as a friend of Jeanne's and gave Maria the letter of introduction. He said he had heard of Maria's amazing testimony from many people and wanted to meet her and hear it for himself. He knew she would have personal details and insights only she could give.

As they stood in the cave entrance, she replied, "Come over here." She pointed to a large, smooth rock. "We can sit here in the sun," she added.

Marcus said, "There is so much I want to know! Where do I begin? How did you come to know Jesus? Tell me about your experiences with his disciples. Why did you come to this region?"

But his primary request was simple, "Tell me about Jesus and about your travels, your experiences with him."

Marcus knew from what he had been told by Jeanne that it would be a spellbinding and lengthy story. Indeed, it was both. The amazing events Maria had experienced over several years with Jesus and his disciples wove a fascinating and inspiring story. Marcus would return to Maria's cave many times over the following months, learning about her life and the teachings of Jesus.

Although Maria was no longer preaching to groups, her friend Jeanne knew she was still inspired to share her many fascinating stories. Maria had been so close to Jesus, having traveled with him and his disciples, that she took his message and ministry personally. She was one of his most devoted followers and had financially supported Jesus and his closest disciples as they traveled around Galilee and Judea.

Even now, Maria's dark eyes sparkled when she talked to visitors, retelling stories of her time with Jesus. She recounted his parables and his message of the coming kingdom of God, urging those present who had not done so, to repent and change their lives. She stressed the imminent coming of the kingdom of God and with it, the final judgment. Her voice was soft and calming but conveyed a sense of authority.

As Maria made herself comfortable on her stone seat, she looked Marcus over carefully. She was impressed by his eagerness and serious demeanor.

After he finished his request Maria said, "So many questions, so much to tell. Not knowing what Jeanne has told you, I will tell you briefly of my life here.

"I have lived in this cave for several years. Originally, I lived in the city with two friends, Salome, and another Maria. A few years ago my friends moved to other towns to spread the gospel there, to many more people."

Maria leaned toward Marcus and said quietly, "Before I begin my story, before you begin asking questions, tell me something about life in Tegulata. Are people well, have there been any widespread illnesses, many deaths? And are the farmers doing well, is the harvest abundant?"

And for a long while, they talked, sharing news and personal experiences. In no time at all they were friends and went on as if they had known each other for years. Once Maria felt comfortable sharing personal stories about herself with Marcus, she began telling of her earlier experiences.

"I delighted in telling people of Jesus, the Jewish Messiah, who came to warn people of the coming judgment of God, the coming of the kingdom of God and the need to repent. I brought many to believe and join the Way."

Soon after she arrived, Maria had a reputation in the area of Tegulata. It was not the usual reputation a foreign woman might expect but one of a woman with a fascinating story and a new religion. When word spread of her presence, large groups of people would gather around her. They came to hear her talk about her life in distant Israel. They also wanted to learn about her new religion and about Jesus, the man at the center of it.

"I moved to this cave when I was no longer strong enough to speak before the large groups that had once followed me. Now I seldom venture beyond the cool shade of the valley. Once a day I walk to a small spring just down the path for water."

Maria relied on pilgrims and generous locals for bread, cheese, fruit, and occasional vegetables to feed her small hunger. Local people remembered her passionate preaching, her spellbinding stories of Jesus and his miracles. Her own life story was an inspiration to many people. Her acts of kindness, compassion and care had touched many of the struggling peasants. In return, local people brought her food and anything else she needed. But her needs and desires were small as she led a life of meditation and prayer.

Maria and Marcus sat on a rock just outside the cave entrance, in the warmth of the morning sun. Marcus offered Maria a small loaf of bread and a piece of cheese he had brought for breakfast. Maria thanked him for the food but ate little. She normally did not eat until noon. Maria suggested that the next time he came to visit, he should come in late afternoon and bring some wine with the bread so they might share a simple ritual as a remembrance of Jesus' life and sacrifice.

Maria began her tale, speaking in a low voice, relating her meeting with Jesus.

She said, "Perhaps I should first tell you how I came to know Jesus, how he changed my life and caused me to travel so far to spread his call to repent.

I heard from neighbors that a charismatic preacher had come close to Magdala, the village where I lived. Having heard of Jesus' profound teachings, I was eager to meet him. I was curious about someone who could attract such attention."

She continued, "Jesus was an itinerant preacher who traveled around Galilee. Because at that time he was so near Magdala, I went with several of my friends to hear him. He was indeed an inspiring speaker. The message Jesus brought from God, his father, was simple. To receive the blessings of God, one must repent and ask forgiveness for one's sins. A person's life must change, whether from serious sins or simple selfishness.

The message of Jesus was love, compassion and giving. He said that one should not be bound by legalistic rules and restrictions in service to God. It is more important to love thy neighbors, love thy enemies. His death and resurrection brought salvation to those who repented and tried to live sinless lives. He also said that the coming of the kingdom of God was at hand, coming within the life times of this generation."

Marcus was struck by the seeming simplicity of Jesus' message: 'Repent and sin no more', and the passion with which Maria spoke. He was also wise enough to know that 'repent and sin no more' was in reality not so simple. But even after their brief meeting he knew Maria's passion held hope it could be done.

Marcus, noting how high the sun had risen, suggested this might be a good time for him to return home. By now the men and women of the village would be busy with chores. They would be harvesting crops and preparing food for winter storage. He, too, had work to do at home. He promised to return soon, perhaps in the afternoon as Maria had suggested.

As Marcus rose to leave, Maria said, "Before you go, I have a question."

Marcus, a bit puzzled, said, "Certainly. You are willing to tell me so much. I will try to answer any question."

Maria asked, "Why did Jeanne urge you to come here? It has been a while since she last sent anyone to visit me."

Marcus, embarrassed, looked down at his feet. "Well... Well, she thought that I was paying too much attention to her young daughter, Claudine. I think she suspected that I did not have the best of intentions. She said nothing about that but took me aside and told me about Jesus. After telling me about many things, she talked of sin, repentance, forgiveness and living a sinless life.

Later, Jeanne took me to meet her friends, also followers of the Way. They were such friendly and caring people that I gladly attended meetings in their homes. I soon became a follower of the Way myself.

I guess just to be sure, Jeanne suggested I come to see you. Jeanne's story of her conversion made me want to come here and learn more about Jesus."

Maria smiled to herself, thinking of Jeanne's cleverness alongside her devotion to her beliefs.

She said, "It has been a long time since I last saw Claudine. She was just a young girl, about so high." She extended her arm, her hand about a meter above the ground. "She was a delightful, clever child."

Marcus quickly added, "She still is. Of course she has grown into a lovely young woman. Like her mother, she is smart and educated."

Maria smiled and said, "Thank you for answering my question. Please give my greetings to Jeanne and her family, especially Claudine."

As Marcus prepared to leave, Maria made one last request. She asked Marcus to join her in a brief prayer. "Heavenly Father," she began. "Bless this man, increase his knowledge, strengthen his belief, bring peace and understanding to him. Help me to tell my story to demonstrate your love and compassion, and the power of your support for your faithful servants. Amen."

"Amen," repeated Marcus. He took Maria's hands in his and thanked her deeply for her willingness to share her story and to bring him closer to Jesus.

Marcus said goodbye and wished Maria a pleasant afternoon.

Marcus had been delighted to be able to sit with Maria and talk as if old friends. She had a way of quickly making people feel like a real friend. Jeanne had told him much about Jesus, but Marcus had questions and was eager to learn more. He wanted even more to hear her story of her time with Jesus, to learn more about Jesus and his activities. He looked forward to seeing her again soon.

Even though Maria was older and less active, she still retained much of her earlier vitality. Marcus could still see her younger self, her vitality and eagerness to share her faith. She had not lost her enthusiasm for spreading the message of repentance and warning of the imminent coming of the kingdom of God. Her mind was still sharp, and she maintained her sense of humor, cheerful attitude, and optimistic outlook. Her spirit was still that of a younger woman.

He was also curious as to how she came to be here in Gaul. He wondered what prompted her to leave her home, friends and other followers of The Way and make such a long, arduous journey. Thinking of his own travel from Italy, he wondered how she made the long journey.

As he retraced his steps along the trail, walking downhill toward the city, he reflected on his brief visit with Maria. He was impressed with her grace, openness, and intelligence. He looked forward to many visits and learning more about her and her experiences with Jesus.

Chapter Two

Growing up in Magdala

It was mid-afternoon when Marcus returned to Maria's cave the following day. It was a beautiful autumn day, the sky a brilliant blue, accented with large, puffy white clouds. The sun illuminated the brilliant colors of the trees and bushes along the small valley. The colors, accentuated by the bright sun, made the walk along the path even more enjoyable.

As Maria had requested, Marcus brought a loaf of freshly baked bread and a flask of wine. Maria smiled, pleased he had remembered. She broke the bread and gave Marcus a piece, saying that it should always be a reminder the last meal Jesus had with his disciples, his death and resurrection and his promise to share meals with them again in the kingdom of heaven.

Maria excused herself and walked quickly to just inside the cave. She brought out two small unglazed ceramic cups and poured some wine in each. This, too, she said should be a reminder of the life of Jesus and an expression of thanks for his sacrifice for everyone's sins.

Maria concluded, "Simple, every day acts such as eating, and drinking should remind us of the life and death of Jesus. They should remind us that we are saved and must live our lives accordingly. Such thoughts are not just for holy days and festivals."

Maria hesitated before resuming her story. Finally she said, "I think it would be best if I gave you some background about myself. My early life will become important later in my tale and it might be easier to go back to the beginning now."

Maria explained to Marcus, "In Galilee, where I was born and raised, people spoke several languages. The local people, being Jews, spoke Aramaic or Hebrew. There were also many Romans and Greeks living in the area and most spoke Greek, although a few used Latin.

Because of its history under Roman rule, many non-Jews had settled in the region. As a result, Galilee was often called 'Galilee of the Gentiles'. Several new cities, such as Sepphoris and Tiberius, were built by the Romans in the decades after I was born.

My parents named me 'Miriam', a common Hebrew name. However, as I traveled farther from home, I found Gentiles used the Greek and Latin name 'Maria'. Even in Judea this was more common than 'Miriam'. Thus I had no objection to being called 'Maria'.

Because Miriam and Maria were common names for girls in that region, people outside Magdala needed a way to distinguish me from all the other Marias and Miriams they knew. Because I was unmarried and from Magdala, I was often referred to as 'Maria of Magdala' or 'Maria the Magdalene'."

Maria began her story at the very beginning. She was born in the small city of Magdala on the western shore of the Sea of Galilee. Her family lived in a small house in a village of similar homes that consisted of several small rooms that adjoined a courtyard. Because of her father's ship building business, their home was on the edge of the city, providing a little more space than homes in the city center.

Magdala was a small city with paved streets and sidewalks. Streets were lined with shops and houses, mostly two-story buildings of stone. Because Magdala was a compact city, there were few open spaces between buildings; a system of underground drains carried waste water to the lake. This drainage system was necessary with so many fish sellers cleaning fish in the city.

"Like all towns and cities around the Sea of Galilee, Magdala was a fishing town with a busy harbor. Most of the men made their living from the sea, primarily as fishermen. Others built or repaired boats, sold fishing supplies, bought, or sold fish, or had other businesses that catered to fishermen. No matter the occupation, the men were always busy and the work hard."

Marcus asked, "How large was the Sea of Galilee? Were all the port cities alike?"

Maria smiled and responded, "The Sea of Galilee is certainly not as large as the Mediterranean Sea, it's actually just a small lake."

Magdala was widely known for its fine salted fish. The dried, salted fish were exported throughout the region. One of the landmarks of the city was the tower used for drying fish. The widespread popularity of the dried fish brought a high level of prosperity to the town.

Maria explained, "Although our lives were not simple, our living arrangements were rather basic. Because homes were small, much of our time was spent outdoors; most of our daily activities were done outside.

Parts of our courtyard were paved with flat stones but most of it was just packed earth. In the courtyard, grain was separated from the chaff and the grain was ground in stone mortars. The courtyard was also where cooking and baking took place. The oven and stove were made of stone and mud bricks.

Because we got so little rain, and it almost never snowed, houses in that region had flat roofs. Some houses had a stairway to the roof and others simply had a ladder leaning against a wall.

We used our roof for many activities. We spread out grapes and figs to dry; raisins and dried figs could then be stored and used in the winter. Certain peppers were also dried and used as spices year-round.

The peppers added flavor to foods that otherwise would be rather bland. Raisins and especially dried figs provided a sweet treat at the end of winter meals when oranges and apples were no longer available.

When the heat of summer made sleeping indoors uncomfortable, we would sleep on the roof. Often there was a breeze at night, which made sleeping outside even better. I always enjoyed lying on my back, staring up at the sky filled with uncountable stars. It was almost a magic feeling, especially when shooting stars streaked across the sky.

We had a small walled garden behind the house, adjacent to the kitchen. There my mother raised herbs and a few vegetables. Of course, grain was grown in larger fields outside the city. The surrounding land was hilly; mostly low, rounded hills with only a few trees.

There are long periods during the year when rain was scarce if it rained at all. The region was arid, and vegetation was sparse. There were few trees, and they mostly grew along rivers and larger streams. Many of the streams were dry much of the year. Water in them was limited to the short rainy season.

Nearly all families owned a donkey or horse. They were used for pulling wagons and plows; a horse could be ridden on longer trips. My family's donkey stayed within the courtyard along with a few chickens. A twisted olive tree grew beside the outer courtyard wall and provided shade for the animals. When I was young, I often played in the shade to escape the heat of the unrelenting sun.

A smaller fig tree grew in a corner of the courtyard. It produced many plump figs that added a sweet treat to end a meal. Our small tree did not produce enough figs to last our family all year, so we got some from neighbors in trade or bought more in the market.

Women were busy much of the day, preparing meals, making or mending clothes and often tending to children. Women of the family — mothers, daughters and older women — sat in the shade to prepare food and to cook, and, of course, socialize.

Much of the land in and around the village was bare, dusty ground. As a consequence, any and every flat surface was covered in a layer of dirt. Women were kept busy dusting tables and work areas in the house. Clothes always seemed to be permeated with dust.

My uncle, my mother's brother, raised sheep on the hills near Magdala and provided us with wool. My mother had to clean the wool and spin it into thread. She then set up a small loom and wove the thread into cloth, which she used to make a warm cloak to wear on cool evenings and in the winter.

If she had excess wool or woolen cloth she would trade for cotton or linen cloth. Usually this was not sufficient for our family needs, so she bought more cloth in the market. All this work, plus sewing and mending, keep women in the family busy between preparing and cooking food and keeping house.

When I was a very young girl, I was taught about work in the kitchen. My mother showed me how to pick only the ripe beans in the garden, how to grind the grain and herbs and how to control the fire beneath a pot by adding just the right amount of wood. Mother taught me to mix flour, water and yeast to make bread and how to judge the temperature of the oven—without burning my hand.

Many of the things my mother taught me were about food and cooking. The life of a woman was quite restricted. The kitchen was her kingdom.

Certain foods were prohibited by tradition but there were practical reasons as well. Because of the very warm climate, many foods spoiled quickly and eating them could make people sick. Also, some meats were unsafe to eat because, with limited wood for fires, they were often not cooked enough, also causing people to become sick.

It was also important to pay attention to what type of pots were used for some purposes. Safe drinking water was not always available which made cleaning pots difficult. Thus ceramic pots easily became contaminated, spreading illness; those made of stone were much safer. We learned from tradition which types of utensils were proper to use.

As I grew older, I often went with my mother to the market. Some of the merchants sold their goods from stalls, simple wooden tables beneath a frayed cloth roof that provided shelter from the hot sun. Others, especially the local farmers, simply spread their goods on blankets on the ground. They wisely chose the shady side of the street to protect their goods and for their own comfort.

In a coastal town the size of Magdala, these vendors would be found extending a block or more along both sides of a street or alley. There were always several merchants offering the same items, whether it was fruit or vegetables, fish or meat, cheese, olives, olive oil or milk.

I learned to look for the freshest and best of any item. I accompanied my mother to the markets every day but the Sabbath to buy fresh fruits and vegetables, bread and milk. At least once a week we visited other markets to buy cheese, olives, olive oil and other less spoilable foods.

I often heard my mother haggle with merchants to get a lower price for what she purchased. She taught me how to choose the best milk or flour, to get fruit that was ripe but not too ripe, and how to judge the ripeness of melons. Outwardly, daily life seemed easy, uncomplicated and relaxed. However, being a wife and mother required many skills and much knowledge."

Maria's well-proportioned face, flowing dark hair, sparkling dark eyes and slender body turned many heads as she walked assuredly through the small town. Young men, from muscular fishermen to carpenters and craftsmen to slender sons of merchants, took notice. They frequently called out, 'salute, Maria' in a flirtatious tone as she passed. She simply smiled and nodded in response.

As Maria reached her mid-teens, she went to the market alone to do the family shopping. Because Maria always knew exactly what she wanted and who usually had the best quality products and the best prices, the merchants she most often dealt with looked forward to her visits. They could count on a pleasant transaction with few questions or quarrels.

Maria's father, Lucas, was a successful ship builder in Galilee. Because he built boats that could not just survive the sudden fierce storms on the Sea of Galilee, but were easy to control, he was in demand by captains and merchants. He was well known for his skilled workmanship, quality materials and reasonable prices. Sailors and merchants around the Sea of Galilee had many connections with their counterparts in distant Mediterranean ports. Thanks to these contacts, Lucas' reputation spread beyond the Sea of Galilee to the broader maritime community. As a consequence, he had contacts along the north coast of the Mediterranean as far west as Spain.

Maria's father — being cosmopolitan — hired the wife of a Roman soldier to teach Maria Greek. That was the language used by educated Romans throughout the empire. She was a serious student and soon had a good knowledge of the language. Because some of the ship owners who came to her father's ship yard spoke Latin, Maria soon understood Latin as well. Knowledge of these languages, in addition to her native Aramaic and Hebrew, proved useful in her later life.

Being part of a family with wide-ranging interests and foreign connections, Maria developed a fascination for the wider world. She enjoyed hearing stories of different cultures, lifestyles and traditions. She learned to listen carefully to conversations in the village, in the market, but especially in the boat yard. Her father's visitors told spellbinding and amazing tales of travel, adventure, and danger. They whetted her desire to travel, to see and experience other cultures for herself. When doing mundane tasks, such as grinding grain, she fanaticized about visiting exotic places.

When Maria was about fifteen, her parents began hinting she should begin looking for a husband. Girls usually married when quite young, sometimes when only thirteen years old.

Whenever Maria visited the shipyard, her father made sure she met the smarter and better-looking young men working there. Maria was very attractive, and her father had no problem getting young men to stop by the office and talk to her.

Maria patiently greeted and talked with each young man her father introduced. It was soon clear, however, to both Maria and the young men, that Maria was very intelligent and possessed great knowledge of many topics while the men, well-schooled by local standards, were no match.

At local festivals and Jewish feast days, Maria was approached by many charming bachelors. Her beauty could be spotted at some distance and mothers often pointed her out to their sons. Many of the men were polite, kind, bright and had decent jobs, but they did not meet Maria's high standards.

It was not too long before Maria was known all over Magdala as a woman who knew too much. An afternoon or evening of conversation with her was stimulating, entertaining and, due to her sense of humor and easy laughter, even fun. But the thought of always being a step behind her intellectually kept even the best of men from desiring a lifetime of inferiority.

As a young woman, Maria often encountered merchants from distant Roman cities who came to Magdala to purchase salted fish for which the city was famous. Her curiosity about distant places, foreign foods and customs led to long conversations with men from many places unlike western Galilee. Maria's knowledge and intelligence impressed the visitors, discouraging their interests in less savory activities and keeping their minds on conversation about shared interests.

Galilee was a restive region and Maria heard whispers of an always impending revolt against the Romans. Although Maria witnessed Roman oppression of the Jews, she appreciated the benefits of the Roman Empire. Her father's ship building business expanded beyond the Sea of Galilee thanks in part to Roman commercial networks.

Marcus was fascinated by Maria's account of her early life in Magdala. In many respects, it was similar to his life, in others, quite different. Many aspects of life in a Roman town in Italy were quite distinct from a village in Galilee. Differences in climate and culture resulted in different house construction, lifestyles, foods and crops. However, having grown up in a small town in central Italy, he could relate to her descriptions of home life and commercial and cultural activities.

Maria, always curious and eager to learn, asked Marcus where he was from, how had he come to Tegulata and how did he earn a living? She also asked if he had family in the area.

Marcus, having asked Maria so many questions, was quite willing to share his story even though it was shorter and certainly not as exciting as hers.

"I came to this region several years ago as a soldier in the Roman army. When my service was completed, I simply remained here. For a while I worked as a carpenter and farm hand. I made sufficient money that, with my military pension, I had a good life. As part of my pension I was given a plot of land here.

While in Italy I had learned about growing grapes and producing wine, so I planted a small field with grape vines. When they began to bear, I modified an olive press and, with the help of some friends from home, established a small winery. Because the soil and climate here are suitable for vineyards, I was successful. Now I ship wine to many Roman cities."

Maria, having been raised in Magdala with its extensive exports of salted fish, could easily relate to Marcus' wine exporting business. She was familiar with the hard manual labor involved and also the complexities of managing a business. She knew of the negotiating skills involved in arranging sales, obtaining ships and men to move large quantities of cargo. She had great admiration for Marcus' abilities and dedication. With such skills, Maria saw Marcus as a potentially important part of the spread of the Way in Gaul. That increased her desire to share the message of Jesus along with her life story.

As the late afternoon air cooled, Maria and Marcus relaxed and shared stories of their families and life at home. They laughed at humorous incidents that occurred within their families and neighborhoods. They also talked of illnesses and the passing of beloved family members and close friends.

Marcus listened carefully, enjoying Maria's ability to make even mundane everyday activities interesting. It was easy to understand how she could have been so successful in explaining the message of Jesus and winning converts. He was sorry when they had to end a day's time together. But time passed quickly, and Marcus had to return home to his increasing business demands.

Marcus was always eager to return to Maria's cave, to hear more of her story. When he came back the next day, Maria picked up her story, telling of her first adventures away from home. She was now old enough and confident enough to travel away from Magdala.

Maria continued her story, "Word spread of a dramatic preacher, shaggy and dressed as a hermit, traveling along the Jordan River. Despite his appearance, he held people spellbound with his preaching." John the Baptizer, as he was called, had been preaching in Judea, a several days' walk from Galilee. Now he was moving north and closer to Magdala, Maria's hometown.

"When John came close to the Sea of Galilee many of my neighbors made the still long and difficult journey to hear him. They were greatly impressed with his talk of the coming kingdom of God and his call to repent. When they returned, they spoke highly of John's elegant — and sometimes fiery — preaching.

As spring arrived and weather improved, several friends and I traveled to the Jordan wilderness to hear John speak. We were eager to hear him for ourselves and learn whether the accounts we had heard about him were true or exaggerated."

Sitting at the edge of the crowd, in the shade of trees growing along the bank of the Jordan River, Maria and her friends listened to John's passionate warning of the imminent coming of the kingdom of God and, with it, the final judgment. With equal passion he urged listeners to repent, ask forgiveness and end their sinful ways. Maria and her friends agreed that the reports they had heard about John were true.

When John concluded preaching at the end of the day, he called for those ready to change their lives to come forward and be baptized. At first only a few stepped forward into the Jordan River, then a dozen more, then a crowd. John blessed each in turn and, pressing on his or her head, pushed them into the water. As they emerged from the water, John steadied them and helped them toward the river bank. People standing along the shore took the hands of the newly baptized and helped them upward on the bank with words of praise.

Maria and her friends conferred briefly, joined hands and waded into the crowd and into the river. The baptism by John, though brief, was an experience unlike any they had ever had before. Emerging from the river after the brief submersion they felt cleansed and warm despite the cool water. Now they were part of the growing community of believers.

Maria said to Marcus, "I was taken by his call to repentance, John's warning of the coming judgment of the living and the dead sent chills down my spine. I considered the Romans beyond salvation but hoped my fellow Jews would heed John's call."

Later that spring Maria and her friends returned to the Jordan valley to hear John speak and meet more of his followers. They sat on a large rock at the edge of the river, talking with other women about John's message and the many people who came to hear him preach.

As they watched John baptize the stream of converts who came forward, they saw John hesitate and refuse to baptize one man who approached him. They wondered who and why, but word quickly spread from those close to John to the surrounding crowd. It was Jesus.

Someone recognized Jesus as being from western Galilee. They had heard him in the synagogue discussing the scriptures. A man standing nearby quickly added that Jesus often disputed the rabbi's interpretation of the texts. Someone near Maria agreed and said that Jesus had a great knowledge of the Torah and the ancient prophets. The man said that some who heard Jesus speak were at first upset that Jesus did not seem to recognize the accepted interpretation of the scriptures, but Jesus showed such knowledge that he usually won over those in attendance.

After a brief discussion, John baptized Jesus. As he came up out of the water, a dove was seen descending and hovering over them as if delivering a blessing from God himself. The crowd suddenly became quiet, aware that something special had just occurred.

As Maria and her friends walked back to the nearby village where they spent the night, they discussed what they had seen and heard. They wondered among themselves what it all meant. Surely what they had observed at the Jordan River had a special significance and would somehow be important for the people of Israel.

Maria paused, recalling her thoughts and impressions of all that had taken place. The pause gave Marcus a moment to absorb what Maria had told him.

Maria continued her story of her personal life, telling Marcus, "Even though my father was a skilled ship builder and knew well the dangers of the sudden storms on the Sea of Galilee, he was caught in a terrible storm and was drowned, along with several experienced sailors."

Maria was devastated by her father's tragic death. The suddenness and finality of her loss was something that always haunted her. She and her father had been so close, from childhood to adulthood. He had always encouraged and instructed her.

After his death, Maria tried valiantly to continue his business, knowing how proud he was of its success and excellent reputation. Despite her great efforts, there were fewer ships to build or repair.

The problem was not with the men who worked at the shipyard. They respected and supported Maria. There was no complaint about taking orders from a woman as they recognized her abilities and good judgment. Besides, she seldom gave orders as the men knew the business and were hard workers and skilled craftsmen. Maria mostly facilitated agreements between customers and workmen. She simply made contracts, ordered supplies, made payments and let the men do their jobs.

The trouble began as new customers came to order a new boat or arrange repairs. When they learned that a woman owned and managed the business, they were reluctant to proceed. Although they had heard of the good reputation of the yard, they had questions and hesitation about putting their lives and those of their sailors in the hands of a woman.

Maria well knew it was a patriarchal world. Men alone had the power and made the decisions. She knew that was wrong but realized she could not change the culture. It would not be changed.

Men who had previously done business with Maria's father and knew Maria had no problem working with her. But engaging new customers was the only way to continue a business and as their numbers declined, Maria had to consider her options.

Her eyes moist with sadness, Maria picked up her story, "When my father died, I inherited the shipyard. I tried to continue the business, working closely with the workers and customers. Having spent so much time there as a young girl, I knew the business well. However, after a few months, I realized men did not like dealing with a woman. I felt I had little choice but to sell the business.

It was actually fortuitous because Jesus had just begun his preaching in Galilee following the murder of John the Baptizer. I now had the freedom and money to follow him wherever he went. God works in strange and mysterious ways."

Over the late fall and early winter, Marcus returned several times to the cave. He brought firewood, a warm cloak, bread and occasionally a skin of wine to commemorate Jesus' last meal with his disciples. He also brought news that he had been baptized into the Way and was now active in the community of believers.

When Marcus came to see her, Maria always had questions of her own. She asked Marcus about individuals she had known in Tegulata, about the growth of the community of believers. She was concerned about the unity and steadfastness of believers within the community of followers. As the community of followers grew, in the diverse population of Gaul, Romans and other immigrants, divergent views arose and had to be resolved.

Marcus said, "I have been observing Jeanne's husband, Donnadu, and his increasing business with the Roman army, supplying them with food — and wine from my presses — as well as other materials they need. He is both expanding and strengthening his relationships with the local people he buys from and his position with the Roman authorities. This combination of contracts and connections will further his career within the regional leadership.

Because of my position as a merchant exporting wine to Roman colonies, I know the importance of such contacts. I am certain Donnadu will do well and go far."

Chapter Three

A Messiah Emerges

Capernaum, located on the northwest shore of the Sea of Galilee, was one of several ports on the lake. Although it was one of the major ports, it was a small town of about 1,500 people. Like most occupations and activities in those days, there was a seasonal routine to the lives of fishermen, but mending nets was a constant part of that routine.

Nets often snagged on floating pieces of wood, even on a rough board on the side of a boat. Often threads simply broke from wear and age. Even a small opening could allow fish to escape.

Andrew sat on an upturned crate; patiently mending the family's fishing nets. Even though his hands were rough and worn, his skilled fingers quickly knotted the nets. Sitting in the shade, a dozen meters from the water, Andrew dug his bare feet into the cool sand. The pleasant feeling relieved, at least a little, the heat of the day.

A slight breeze blowing along the shore also brought some relief from the afternoon heat. The gentle lapping of the waves on the shore made a relaxing, rhythmic sound. Andrew could also hear his older brother, Peter, down on the shore, disputing something with another boatman.

Like their father and grandfather before him, Andrew and Peter were fishermen on the Sea of Galilee. Andrew, the younger brother, was in his early twenties, strong and muscular as his profession demanded. He was patient and skilled at mending nets as well as sailing their small boat. As a good businessman, he enjoyed bargaining with merchantss, always getting a good price for the family's catch.

Although Peter shared his brother's physical attributes, he did not share his temperament. Andrew was calm, thoughtful, and attentive, while Peter was impetuous, brash, stubborn, and prone to loud outbursts. Peter's mind often seemed to be elsewhere, not on what he was saying.

While Andrew sat mending nets, Timothy, a long-time friend approached, pulled another crate into the shade and joined him. After they had exchanged greetings, Timothy, having not seen Andrew for several days, asked where he had been.

Andrew said enthusiastically, "As spring weather warmed into summer, word reached those of us living on this side of the Sea of Galilee that a fiery new prophet was preaching in the wilds along the Jordan River. We heard from many people about John the

Baptizer and his message; 'Repent, for the kingdom of God is at hand!'

"My brother Peter had little interest in such wild talk, had no desire to make the long walk to the Jordan Valley and be surrounded by large crowds. I was intrigued and went several times to hear John preach. His message of the coming final judgment is a bit frightening but the promise of the coming of the kingdom of God was more promising and gave us hope for a better life."

Timothy nodded and said, "I've heard of this man John. They say his preaching is pretty dramatic. How many times did you go there? Do many people come to hear him? Do they like what he says?"

Andrew replied, "Because of the long distance and difficult path between here and the Jordan Valley, it is a several days' journey. And, of course, I must help my father and Peter with fishing and other tasks, so I only heard John speak a few times. Nevertheless, I considered myself his follower now. With our people living under Roman oppression and the empire wide turmoil, the cry, 'Repent, the kingdom of God is at hand!' struck a chord with me and with many others."

Timothy stood and said, "Speaking of helping with the fishing, I must get back to my family. Some time we must talk more about this prophet and his preaching. I also want to know more about this kingdom of God." With that he turned and walked along the shore, treading on the wet sand near the water for easier walking.

When word came of the killing of John the Baptizer at the order of Herod Antipas, Andrew was shocked, angry, and dismayed. It was another reminder of the brutal oppression by the Romans. The Jewish scriptures told of other prophets long ago who met a tragic end before their prophecies came true. But their prophecies had eventually been fulfilled; their message against greed, immorality and sin were justified. Andrew hoped the fulfillment of John's prophecies would likewise take place soon. He longed for the end of oppressive Roman rule over the Jews.

Not too long after learning of the murder of John the Baptizer, Andrew heard rumors of a new prophet preaching John's message. Some even said the new teacher was the long-awaited Messiah. Andrew was curious and interested, eager to hear someone continuing John's apocalyptic message. When Andrew encountered travelers and merchants from the Jordan valley, he asked for any news of the new prophet.

Jesus had picked up the mantle of John the Baptizer, his slightly older cousin, and continued the call for repentance and warning of the imminent coming of the kingdom of God. However, Jesus eschewed the hard life of the wilderness and preferred to preach in the villages and small towns. He did not take his message to the rugged Jordan valley as John had, but to the area around the Sea of Galilee. Jesus differed from John in other ways as well. He did not dress in the ascetic hair shirt that John had worn, but in the style of most Galileans.

Although John had attracted large crowds, he had not established a group of followers who stayed with him. Nor did John select a few men to work closely with him, sharing his ministry. Those he baptized returned home, desiring to live the life called for by their repentance while they waited for the coming judgment. Jesus, on the other hand, ultimately did gather a group of followers who stayed with him for long periods. And he chose a small group of disciples who remained with him throughout his ministry, learning from him and assisting him as they went.

Jesus and his disciples shared a similar upbringing in small towns around Galilee. Most had the same profession; they were fishermen. Thus they shared stories about families, experiences, joys, and sorrows. They could gather, eat, drink, laugh and support one another.

Jesus and his small band of dedicated followers often walked for days along dusty back roads between small villages, and spent many nights huddled wherever they could find shelter. Their clothes were as dusty as were their bodies and hair. It was only when they reached a large town where they could bathe in a pool, wash their clothes, and perhaps even get their hair and beards trimmed. It was only because their unkempt appearance was so common among the rural population, that Jesus and his company did not turn people away.

Romans, known for their large public baths, were fastidious about cleanliness and appearance. As a result, Romans preferred the larger cities and avoided smaller villages. The local villagers had no objection to their absence.

Occasionally Jesus and his companions stayed in a disciple's hometown such as Capernaum and Bethsaida. When such opportunities arose, they might stay for a week or more, taking advantage of better accommodations and home-cooked meals.

Timothy, like all fisherman on the Sea of Galilee, had frequent contact with others in his trade. Some of their contacts were about business but often it was purely social. One day, as Andrew and Peter pulled their boat onto the beach, Timothy called them over to join him in the shade. Andrew and Peter appreciated a break from their labor and a chance to visit with a friend. Timothy asked about their families and the size of their catch. Their conversation quickly fell into the normal pattern of old friends meeting with old friends.

Timothy offered them bread and wine and asked, "Have you had an opportunity to hear Jesus preach? I understand he has traveled north along the shore of the Sea of Galilee to Capernaum."

Andrew eagerly replied, "Yes, last week I took an afternoon off from fishing to hear this new preacher. Although his message of the coming kingdom of God and his call to repent is much like that of John the Baptizer, Jesus has a different style of preaching. Jesus is more personal, telling stories to which each person in the crowd could relate, stories about everyday activities and people like us.

His calm manner, encouraging people to repent without threatening them, appealed to many listeners and the crowds following him are growing larger. Even his message about the coming of the kingdom of God and the final judgment was one of promise, not doom." Returning home, Andrew told Peter, "Tomorrow you must go with me to hear him speak."

Andrew continued, "We both went to hear Jesus and he really impressed us; his encouragement to care for others inspired us. A few days ago, Jesus was walking on the shore of the lake and stopped to talk with us. As we sat on our boat, he asked us about our families, our lives, and our beliefs. He was very friendly and seemed just like one of us. For someone who attracts large crowds, he was quite humble.

After talking with us a while, he asked Peter and me to travel with him, to learn more about the coming kingdom and how to convince others to repent and follow his way. When Jesus returns in a few days, we will go with him."

Timothy could hardly believe what Andrew had said. He asked incredulously, "How can you leave your business, your families and all you have to follow this man? I understand he is an inspiring, impressive speaker. But to leave everything to follow him… For how long?"

After a moment of silence, Andrew replied, "We don't know how long. He says the kingdom of God will come soon, so perhaps not too long. But with time short, we must call all Jews to repent."

They sat in silence for a while before Timothy rose, patted Andrew on the shoulder and said, "You are a good man and courageous. I couldn't do it; I can't leave my family and my work. I wish you well and will help look after your family. Please send me word of your travels and activities. When Jesus comes back to this area, I'll certainly come to listen to him and to see you."

Timothy and Andrew hugged, wished each other well and said goodbye as Timothy turned toward town and Andrew returned to his boat.

Andrew was the first to be called by Jesus to be one of his closest followers. Jesus had heard that Andrew had been a follower of John the Baptizer and a firm believer in the coming kingdom of God. Peter was more of a 'rock' to Andrew's 'polished stone', but Jesus saw potential in Peter, and asked both brothers to follow him.

The men chosen as disciples were not randomly selected. They were not men who, on sudden impulse, decided to drop everything, leave their families and professions and follow some stranger who said, "Follow me." They were men he had known from around the Sea of Galilee and who had heard him speak in the synagogue. These were men who liked what he said.

In addition to the twelve disciples, a group of serious followers, men, and women, numbering perhaps ten or fifteen, traveled with Jesus everywhere. They always sat with the disciples, close to Jesus so they could hear every word. They listened intently and often asked Jesus questions after the locals had returned home at the end of the day. Some of Jesus' sayings, especially his parables, often needed explanation.

After traveling with Jesus for about a year, Andrew returned home to visit his parents. While there, he visited his friend Timothy, finding him perched on the bow of his boat, mending nets. Andrew hailed him and walked over and greeted his friend with a big hug. He asked if he could help spread the net so Timothy could see places that needed repair.

Andrew eagerly told him of all the things Jesus said and did. He talked of Jesus' concern for those in need and his miracles that healed sickness, blindness and even leprosy. Timothy listened intently, asking about the crowds and the reactions among the people.

Andrew said, "People were always curious, sometimes doubtful but usually interested and polite. Frequently a few priests or synagogue elders came to ask questions, hoping to embarrass Jesus or to dispute with him. Jesus seemed to enjoy refuting their arguments. His knowledge of the scriptures is superior to theirs."

As Andrew finished his account of the previous year, Timothy said, "I heard that there are women among the followers of Jesus. Is that true? Are they among his closest followers? What do they do? Do they just cook and serve the men, or do they participate in his ministry?"

Andrew was well aware of the traditional roles women played and their place in local society. He noted that although Roman society allowed women many rights, local society was male dominated. Andrew also noticed that Jesus clearly did not hold these traditional attitudes. Jesus often spoke to women and healed them just as he did men. Despite the strong local tradition, Jesus welcomed young woman among his followers.

Andrew replied, "Yes, women are among his followers, a few even among his closest followers. Jesus treats everyone the same, men and women, poor and rich. However, some of the disciples, especially my brother Peter, are clearly not happy to have Jesus frequently conversing with women."

Andrew paused and then added, "As an example of how Jesus welcomed women, let me tell you about a woman named Maria. We had stopped at a house near Magdala where a couple had invited us to eat with them. I was sitting at the table with the other disciples, listening to Jesus. Two women, Maria, and Salome, were friends of the host and were helping in the kitchen. Maria came into the room and was placing plates on the table when something Jesus said caught her attention. She pulled up a bench, sat down and listened intently.

After a few minutes, Peter said, "Uh, Maria, shouldn't you be helping in the kitchen?"

Jesus said, "Relax, Simon. Work in the kitchen is nearly done. Maria is a very good woman who will become a devoted follower and will work hard for my mission. She is welcome to join us." So Maria was allowed to remain with us. She traveled with us for a long time after that and often sat at Jesus' feet, listening, and asking questions. Maria even provided money to buy food and other supplies for the disciples."

Andrew unfolded more of the net Timothy was mending, spreading it over his lap.

Timothy asked, "If this Maria from Magdala was such a devoted follower and contributed money to support the group, why wasn't she chosen to be a member of the twelve?"

Andrew responded, "I wondered that myself and I asked Jesus why only men were chosen to be disciples. Jesus explained that the reasons he only chose men to be his closest disciples were simple. Men traveling together attracted no suspicious attention. However, unmarried men and unmarried women under the same circumstances would invite scurrilous rumors.

He also said that men could sleep in the open or in rude shelters, whereas women would be reluctant to sleep out of doors or in the common crude inns where we sometimes stayed. Perhaps more important, Jesus said the twelve disciples would eventually judge the twelve tribes of Israel and Jesus knew no tribe would submit to judgment by a woman.

Even if women were not chosen to be among the twelve, many women followed Jesus. Some only joined the crowds when Jesus was near their villages. Others might rejoin the group for several days while Jesus was within a region where the women might have relatives. A few, like Maria Magdalene and her close friends, Salome, and Maria, stayed with Jesus throughout his ministry."

Timothy hopped off the boat, stretched his legs and turned to Andrew and asked, "You said sometimes large crowds came to hear Jesus. I heard that thousands came. Did that really happen? What about when you were traveling from town to town?"

Andrew replied, "Big crowds, perhaps several hundred people, might come when we were near a large city. Crowds were sometimes big but often only ten or twenty came out to listen."

Andrew continued, "Jesus and the disciples awoke early, especially when we slept outdoors as the early sunshine and animal sounds reached our senses. After a simple breakfast, we selected an open space near the edge of town where people could gather.

People usually began to gather around Jesus early in the morning, after tending to their necessary morning chores, arriving early to avoid the heat of late afternoon.

Early in the day the air was pleasant, often carrying the fragrances of newly mown hay, citrus fruits, flowers, or other earthy smells. If we were near the Sea of Galilee, as we often were, the many smells of the sea enveloped us. It was a pleasant time as well as exciting. We all felt great times lay ahead.

Those coming to hear Jesus were from all levels of society, from peasants to public officials. True, it was more of the former than the latter, but all were there, all were welcome. Even sinners, answering Jesus' call, did not stay away."

Andrew added, "I usually stood near the road as I enjoyed greeting those coming to hear Jesus. I often inquired about their home towns or occupations. I was sometimes amazed at the differences in wealth, status, and variety of occupations of people in the crowd. Jesus attracted people from all walks of life.

As the crowd dispersed at the end of the day, Jesus, the disciples, and perhaps a few others, returned to our camp and gathered around a fire to eat and discuss the day's activities. I sometimes asked Matthew for his estimate of the number of people in the crowd. Matthew was good with numbers. It came with his profession, I guess. If Matthew didn't have a number, he would have a comment, making comparisons with previous crowds.

The number of people coming to hear Jesus preach varied from day-to-day. In part it depended on the weather, where they were in the yearly agricultural cycle, how near Jesus and his close followers were to villages and towns. Sometimes, only a dozen or so of the local people turned out, but other days it might be hundreds. Of course, Matthew and I were always pleased to report a greater number to Jesus."

Timothy rolled up the string he used to mend his nets, stood, folded the net, and placed it in the small boat, ready for the evening sail on the lake.

He looked appraisingly at Andrew and said, "You are part of a great movement. Everyone I talk with claims Jesus is changing the lives of many Jews in Galilee and Judea. Some believe him to be the Messiah who will free this region from Roman rule. All speak of the coming kingdom of God, even if they are not certain what that means. Regardless of what that actually means, Jesus has many supporters in Galilee."

Andrew stood to leave and rejoin Jesus and the other disciples for dinner.

He hugged his friend and said, "Thank you for the good report and your encouragement. Tomorrow we leave to continue our mission of good works and preaching repentance. I hope to see you again, perhaps in the new kingdom."

With another hug, Andrew turned and walked back to town in the calm of early evening twilight.

Chapter Four

Maria and Her Friends Join Jesus

During the months that followed, Marcus returned to Maria's cave as often as he could. Sometimes, only a few days passed between his visits, at other times a week intervened because his business demanded his attention. Maria's stories were spellbinding, and she told them in such vivid and engaging language that he could easily picture the places and people she described. Marcus found it difficult to stay away for very long.

Marcus was not only drawn to Maria by her fascinating stories about her life but by the enjoyment of simply visiting with her. Her engaging personality and broad knowledge made discussing even everyday life, everyday people and events enlightening and enjoyable. Marcus also realized Maria was no ordinary woman. He was enthralled by her stories and amazed by her uncommon abilities.

Marcus eagerly made the walk from the city to her isolated cave, always wondering what other interesting tales she might share. During his walks he had time to contemplate the meaning and significance of her accounts of Jesus and his message of salvation. The walk, although up hill and steep in some places, was not unpleasant. The shade of the trees, the sounds of the stream beside the path and songs of the many birds produced a mood for meditation.

The stories she shared were more than mere travel accounts and descriptions of events, fascinating as they were. Although she didn't emphasize it, her stories also told of a brave and adventuresome woman, one devoted to preparing people for the coming judgment. Maria was so humble that her dedication, intelligence, and knowledge were hidden.

Maria's voice was not powerful like that of a sailor who had to be heard above a storm or a general who had to be heard above the sound and chaos of a battle. But her voice was strong and clear. It was easy to understand how she could preach to a large group and, with her personal message about Jesus, be convincing and inspiring. Although Latin was not her native language, she spoke it with conviction. She learned it as a child and used it more and more as she traveled west. She spoke it like a Roman, although with a slight accent, having now lived in Gaul for many years.

Traveling to Gaul had been no problem language-wise for Maria as she traveled on Roman and Greek ships. Once there she encountered local people who spoke still another language. Gaul had been a Roman province for over 150 years so there were many Latin speakers in some areas as Roman soldiers, merchants and families moved to the region. There also were bilingual speakers among both the Romans and local residents. Maria was intelligent, had a gift for languages and quickly learned to communicate with all the people she met.

On still another pleasant, sunny afternoon, Marcus made his journey to Maria's underground home. She greeted him warmly and they took their seats on the now familiar low, rounded boulders. After chatting and sharing news of the city and of several recent visitors to her cave, Maria continued recounting her story to Marcus.

"Two of my close friends, Salome, and Maria, and I joined the crowds walking out into the countryside to listen to Jesus. At first, we went only when he was within half a day's walk of Magdala. But soon, convinced of his promise of salvation and his warning of the imminent coming of the judgment and kingdom of God, 'within the lifetime of those people here', we began going farther from Magdala. Because I had money from the sale of my father's shipyard, I could afford to buy food and pay for lodging in the small inns in towns near where Jesus was speaking.

With the money I made from the sale of my father's business, I was also able to help finance Jesus and his disciples. Even though they lived frugally, owned little and often slept in the open or in the homes of supporters, there were always expenses. Sometimes they needed to buy food, sandals or rarely, even a new cloak.

Many evenings, most of the people following Jesus left to return home or, if far from home, to find places to sleep. Often only Andrew, John, Peter, Matthew, I and perhaps a few others remained, sitting around the campfire. We discussed the teachings of Jesus and the reactions of the crowds, the coming apocalypse and the following thousand years of peace and justice. I often talked with Andrew because, like me, he had been a follower of John the Baptizer.

I always enjoyed these opportunities to be close to Jesus. I was able to learn details of his message he couldn't share with the poorly educated crowds. Often the meaning of what he said was plain, such as 'Blessed are those who mourn for they shall be comforted'. But other times his explanation of scripture, especially Isaiah, held a deeper, less obvious meaning."

Maria paused, considering what part of her many layered life story to tell next. It had been a life of adventure and great purpose; certainly not what a little girl in Magdala might have anticipated or even imagined.

Marcus told Maria what he already knew. "Our friend Jeanne shared with me — and with many others

— the teachings of Jesus which you had shared with her. Jeanne is a persuasive person and convinced me of the need to repent and of the coming of the kingdom of God."

"But Jeanne said that you knew Jesus well, traveled with him, shared meals with him and were close to him and heard him speak many times. You saw him heal and comfort many people. More importantly, you saw him when he had risen from the dead."

"Yes, all those things are true," Maria said. "I was the first person to see Jesus following the resurrection. I was the one who told his disciples and other followers that he was raised from the dead." Maria paused, reliving in her mind the joy and amazement she felt at those world-changing events.

Marcus sat for a few moments, trying to analyze, to understand what Maria said. He found the idea of resurrection a bit strange, even if it was somewhat similar to the cult of Isis, an Egyptian religion spread by the Romans. He also found it difficult to believe that he was sitting here with such an amazing person. He was quite overwhelmed at times by that realization, but her relaxed, casual attitude always put him at ease.

Finally, Marcus said, "I'm eager to hear your whole story. I will come back often to listen if you are willing to share it with me."

Maria replied, "I'll be glad to tell you all you want to know, and I hope you will be willing to continue sharing the story with others. It is important that all the world learns about Jesus, his life, death, and resurrection. The kingdom of God may come any day and people must be prepared."

Marcus said, "Before we begin the long story of your relationship with Jesus and his teaching, could you tell me about Jesus. He must have been an impressive figure, someone who immediately attracted attention."

She responded, "No, he wasn't an impressive man who stood out in a crowd. He was of average height, neither thin nor fat. His body was strong, firm but not muscular like some of his disciples. He didn't have to pull heavy nets of fish into a boat or lift heavy timbers or stones. But he could easily, with one hand, raise an ill or crippled man to his feet.

Jesus' face was not strikingly beautiful but had a pleasant appearance, his dark eyes shone, and he frequently smiled. He had a keen sense of humor and enjoyed a joke. He could easily relieve tension with a clever remark. I saw him do so several times. His opponents sometimes just shrugged but some responded with a faint smile and a handshake.

His voice was remarkable. It was calm and soothing. He could be heard by a large crowd without shouting. He could speak in a normal voice, or even softly, and be heard by those in the back of the crowd.

Jesus was very intelligent, but he never boasted; he was very humble. He knew the scriptures well, both what they said and what they meant. He understood the feelings and needs of the people he encountered. He knew their sins and also their goodness. He saw the pain in people's faces, their eyes, and sought to comfort them.

Jesus was a wonderful person to be with, to listen to and to watch. Everything he did and said seemed to have a purpose. We never knew what the next day would bring, what we might experience. Every day I was with him I felt a great blessing.

Jesus felt an urgency to call the Jews to repent, to follow more closely their covenant with God. Like the prophets of Hebrew Scriptures, the prophets of ancient days, Jesus warned of the day of judgment. He wanted Israel to live up to its side of the covenant, to regain its place as the people of God."

Maria gazed up into the trees, thoughtfully watching a bird soar in the blue sky.

Marcus was, of course, impressed and sat quietly contemplating all she had said. Finally he said, "I can understand how you were drawn to follow this inspiring man and how he could convince many people to change their lives. It is easy to see how those he chose as disciples, those he asked to follow him and to devote their lives to spreading his message, would do so.

But now you must tell me of the disciples and others close to Jesus. You spent so much time with them you must have known their thinking, what motivated them. To have left family and friends, jobs — everything — they must have been quite different from most people. What were his disciples like? What led them to do something so unexpected, so bold?"

Maria thought for several minutes and said, "Where to begin? Simon Peter was the most memorable, for good reasons and bad reasons. He was very devoted to Jesus and to spreading the message of the coming kingdom. He saw this movement as ending the Roman control of the Jews and was eager to make that happen. Peter could be loud and often offended people, especially women. He was not happy to have women among the closest followers, even though several of us provided money to support the group. He and I often disagreed and argued.

Peter's brother, Andrew was much more pleasant and agreeable than Peter. He was a fisherman and was from Bethsaida as were a couple of the other disciples. He was gregarious and friendly, agreeable, and cheerful. I enjoyed his company, talking with him often to learn about the mood of the local people, his thoughts about what Jesus said and how people reacted."

Maria smiled to herself, thinking about the contrast between the two brothers.

She then continued, "Thomas was a twin and thus often called Didymus. His twin brother remained at home to work with their father. It is common that a family business was passed from one generation to the next. Thomas was very devoted but full of questions. More than the others, Thomas seemed to have periods of doubt. Despite this he was a serious follower of Jesus."

Marcus said, "These seem like common people, fishermen and laborers. Were any of them educated or public speakers? How did Jesus expect them to preach and spread his message? You're a gifted speaker and have convinced many. But what of the other followers?"

Maria appreciated his compliment but did not want to make comparisons. She said, "Most of the disciples, like most rural people of Galilee, were uneducated. Matthew was an exception. He could read, write, and calculate taxes at least well enough to accumulate a wealth well beyond that of the common people. Because he collected taxes for the Roman authorities, and a little more for himself, he was disliked by the local people. But because he was knowledgeable, I enjoyed talking with him. His abilities went well beyond numbers. He had a deep understanding of people. This ability was very important as we tried to convince people to repent, to follow the teachings of Jesus.

John and James were the sons of Zebedee, apparently a loud man, because James and John were known as the 'sons of thunder'. Some referred to them as somehow a little different from the others, but I thought them typical of most people in the region.

Perhaps they were a little more educated, a little more literate. Some, in fact all of the disciples, were smart, skilled in their profession and could communicate with everyone. John and James were sociable and outgoing. Jesus knew the importance of these qualities. He also recognized their acceptance of outsiders, a feeling not shared by everyone.

"John was a good friend of Peter and they worked closely together. They were a strange pair because they were so different in attitude and behavior. Peter was rough, loud, and outspoken. John was quieter and more thoughtful. Peter often spoke out before he thought things through, which often got him into arguments. John tried, with little success, to calm Peter and to restrain his loud outbursts. Because they were so different, I sometimes thought their interactions were almost amusing."

Maria paused and counted on her fingers. She looked seriously at Marcus and said, "Well, that is six, half of them. They were the most prominent, the best known of the twelve. That will give you a good idea of what the disciples were like. It was an interesting group of people to live with, travel with and to share the experiences of being with Jesus. We all did so much, learned so much and accomplished so much together. We tried hard to prepare the people for the coming final judgment and the coming kingdom. Soon it will be up to God."

She paused again, reliving in her mind some of the many experiences she shared with the disciples. She finally continued, "My relationship with Jesus was in many ways close and personal, more than just another follower of a great and inspiring teacher."

Maria relaxed, almost smiled, and continued, "I should also mention Maria, the mother of Jesus. I met her for the first time at a large wedding at Cana. There must have been a hundred people there but none I recognized. I was never sure who or how someone in our group was related to the bride or groom.

Jesus and his friends stayed on the edge of the gathering, standing near the food and wine preparation area. We talked among ourselves, commenting on the people and the festivities. At one point Jesus' mother, also named Maria, came and sat beside me. She was a quiet person, almost shy. We talked about my travels with Jesus, about his followers and the reactions of people who came to hear him speak. We talked about families and weddings.

She hesitated and then asked me if I had ever thought about marrying Jesus. I said, 'Of course.' However, I quickly added that being married to Jesus would complicate things greatly. I explained that my relationships with some of the disciples were already strained and being married to Jesus would only make matters worse.

Maria was silent for several minutes and then confided that, as any mother would, she wanted Jesus to find a wife. Jesus' mother said that Jesus was thirty years old; he needed to get married, settle down and start a family She hoped he might meet one of the lovely young women in the wedding crowd. She wished he was not so shy, staying out of the crowd and not mingling more. She hoped something might happen to make him noticed, especially by the young women.

After a bit, Jesus' mother excused herself and joined the throng. I had a feeling she had something in mind.

It was just a little later that Jesus' mother convinced Jesus to produce more wine for the party. She had overheard someone frantically tell the head steward they were nearly out of wine. Jesus told his mother that was not his problem, but she insisted that he save the groom the great embarrassment. Jesus finally gave in, changing water into wine. Jesus tried to keep his involvement quiet; he was almost embarrassed by the act. His mother, on the other hand, discretely spread the word that her son produced the superior wine...

Jesus soon returned to our group, and we quietly slipped away. He never told us how he produced the wine and never mentioned meeting any young women."

From the very beginning of her association with Jesus, Maria was a devoted follower. She was smart, better educated than most, thoughtful and curious. She was a serious listener, often inquiring about details and deeper meanings of what Jesus said.

Maria's friendly and outgoing personality allowed her to overcome the patriarchal attitudes of her male companions. She was able to make deep and long-lasting friendships with many of them. As a woman, Maria often had ideas and approaches unlike those of the male disciples. She had a talent for convincing at least some of them to accept her own views and ideas.

But Maria knew she had to be careful. She tried to simply encourage, to suggest actions. If it was too obvious she was trying to lead there would be resentment and a refusal to act. Sometimes she was able to plant a seed, an idea in the mind of an accepted leader and allow him (it was always a him), to persuade the others, to take the credit.

Maria always discussed her thoughts with Jesus first, before sharing them with the disciples. He always approved of her ideas and encouraged her. He frequently praised Maria privately for when he did so in front of the men, some complained and grumbled.

Maria was not pushy or assertive, but she eagerly sought to be close to Jesus, to hear every word he spoke. She frequently managed to sit close to Jesus when he and his closest followers gathered away from the crowds for serious discussions. She knew her presence upset a few of the men no matter how circumspect she was.

"I often sat in front of Jesus but slightly to one side. I had to be careful not to sit too close to Jesus' feet because some of the men did not approve. On some occasions, Peter and a few others would quickly sit down in a line immediately in front of Jesus so I couldn't get close. I could only sit as near as possible and listen carefully.

Once, as I moved to sit near Jesus, Peter attempted to stop me. He stood right in front of me; almost knocking me over. Jesus said, 'Peter, you worry too much about little things. Relax! Mary has chosen a good place which shouldn't be taken from her.' Peter muttered something under his breath and sat down directly in front of Jesus. It was so minor, so petty, but just the beginning of a battle."

Although Maria ignored the many slights by several of the disciples and overlooked their negative comments, she felt them deeply. She and the other close followers of Jesus — even Peter — were working together to spread Jesus' message, to bring as many as possible to the Way and salvation. In a practical sense, such division could confuse possible converts. Knowing this, the complaints and even threats by Peter troubled her greatly.

Regardless of where she sat, Maria made certain she could hear everything and quietly ask questions. She was constantly inspired by the teachings of Jesus. Maria was impressed with Jesus' insights into the lives of the people and their place in the coming kingdom of God.

"As a child, I learned to be a good listener, to ask thoughtful questions and comprehend complex arguments. Because of this training I think I had a better understanding of what Jesus said than many of the others who followed him."

Jesus refused to have favorites among his disciples. He rebuked some when they asked who would sit on his right hand in the kingdom. However, he did admire Maria the Magdalene more than the other disciples, primarily because she had a better understanding of his mission and of his message. She understood nuances that the men often did not. Even after being told several times by Jesus about the coming crucifixion and resurrection, the disciples failed to understand clearly what was happening and what it meant.

"I tried hard to learn and understand all I could from this brilliant, inspired teacher. I was encouraged by Jesus' approval and acceptance of me as a devoted follower. He could clearly see that my knowledge and understanding often exceeded that of the chosen twelve. Or at least I felt that acceptance was real."

Maria continued her explanation of what she learned. "Jesus was not interested in creating an organization; there was no need or time. He sought only to bring people to salvation, draw them into the kingdom of God. The disciples were simply to spread the message, to take this gospel to the ends of the earth.

Jesus' call to repent and his message of the coming kingdom of Heaven — within our lifetime he said — sometimes seemed more dire than thrilling. The warning echoed that of John the Baptizer. But Jesus' message of forgiveness, compassion and salvation resonated with many and drew people to him.

Jesus taught that his followers were not to develop laws and restrictions. Theirs was not to be a legalistic society. The Jews were restricted at every turn by rules and laws that said, 'Don't do this and don't do that'. Jesus taught that one should not simply follow rules for the sake of following rules. He stressed in words and actions that salvation comes from the spirit of the law."

Jesus, his twelve disciples and numerous other followers traveled around the country, mostly in Galilee, urging people to repent and live more compassionate lives. Jesus' message was persuasive but the healings he performed convinced many more to change their lives. His miracles convinced even the most ardent doubters of his powers, that his message came from God.

"At times we moved often, walking from one village to another. The villages and small towns are not far apart and are connected by well-worn trails. Only a few of the larger, more important towns are connected by paved Roman roads. The land is hilly but not rugged and trails follow the easiest routes. Travel isn't difficult and we encountered many people as we walked between villages.

Villages are usually only three or four hours apart. If necessary, a person can walk to a neighboring town, conduct business, or visit family or friends and return home before dark. Traveling in the morning and evening also avoided the heat of the midday. This was especially important in most areas where there was little shade.

As followers of Jesus, we traveled with him around the area and thought little of the time and distances involved. We often talked as we went, which made time pass quickly, made the journey seem even shorter.

After several weeks of traveling from village to village, Jesus, his twelve disciples and a small number of apostles, including myself, usually returned to Capernaum. There we relaxed, talked of our successes and failures, and planned for our next mission.

Some of the followers took advantage of the break and returned home to visit families and catch up on the news. Many had lived around the Sea of Galilee and so it was only a short boat ride to their home village. I remained in Capernaum with Jesus and several others. After a week or so, Jesus called his disciples back.

Jesus, feeling the need to reach many more people, to call more Jews to repent and more closely follow God, sent the twelve disciples into the Galilean countryside to spread his message. It wasn't a complicated message; it was one familiar to the Jews. It was the message of his cousin John the Baptizer, to repent, to prepare for the coming kingdom of God. Jesus instructed them, commissioned them and gave them powers to heal and forgive.

They were gone nearly a month before returning to Capernaum where Jesus waited. They were in good spirits, reporting that many people believed and were baptized. Talking among themselves, however, some admitted to being unwelcome in some synagogues and encountering many people who didn't believe.

Later, feeling more urgency, Jesus sent a larger group of his most dedicated followers to do the same. Most of them were men but I and several of the other women who followed Jesus and provided for him were included. I was excited and overjoyed to be chosen and eagerly went with high expectations.

Just as he sent out his disciples in pairs, he sent those in the larger group by twos. Thus I was able to travel with my close friend Salome."

Maria smiled, recalling those exciting and hopeful days. After a minute she said, "Before we left, Jesus took me aside and quietly told me he knew I would be safe and successful. He said that because I was so familiar with his call to repentance and his promise of forgiveness, I would have no problem winning converts. He also gave me the same powers he gave his disciples to heal."

Like the twelve disciples before them, the men in the larger group spoke to Jews in local synagogues and other places where Jews met. It wasn't possible for Salome and me to speak in synagogues, so we talked to people in markets and other gathering places.

The men Jesus sent traveled in Judea or Galilee. Salome and I moved north along the Mediterranean coast. Eventually we reached Antioch and then turned east to Damascus. We preached to merchants and sailors as well as local residents. We spoke to Jews of course but also Romans, Greeks, and other pagans.

When we returned and rejoined Jesus, other retuning missionaries and those who hadn't been sent, I told Jesus of our success in winning followers. Jesus said, 'Well done Maria. I had great faith that you would convert many.'

Jesus called me out, showing his appreciation and support. He placed his hands on my shoulders and pulled me closer. He kissed me on the mouth. I don't exactly know why that kiss seemed so special. Followers of the Way greeted each other with a kiss. It symbolized the sharing of the Spirit. But those were usually just a touch of the lips, and this was much more than that. It also lasted a second or two longer than the usual kiss. Whatever it was, I felt it deep inside. Jesus took his hands from my shoulders, and I just stood there a minute before saying, softly, 'Thank you.' Jesus simply smiled at me."

Abruptly someone loudly yelled, 'Jesus!' It was Peter, standing at some distance. Jesus nodded his head and said, 'I guess I'd better go see what is bothering Simon now.'"

Maria blushed. "I've never told anyone that. The memory, the feeling just came back so strong." She sat quietly, closed her eyes, and enjoyed the memory.

After a pause, Maria lowered her head and looked at the ground. She said quietly, "As I mentioned, followers of Jesus used a kiss to symbolize love for one another and sharing the Spirit. That was why it was ironic and so hateful for Judas to use a kiss to betray Jesus."

She shifted on the stone seat, looked back at Marcus, and continued, "Even though Jesus never mentioned it, I secretly hoped he was the Messiah who would overthrow the Romans. The people of Galilee, more than Jews elsewhere, longed for the expected Messiah who would free the Jews from Roman domination. Years earlier, several men had appeared among us, claiming to be the Messiah. But they all came to a sudden and sad end at the hands of the Romans, dashing the hopes of the people. Jesus made no such claims, but many people of Galilee hoped Jesus was the true Messiah, the future liberator of the Jews."

It seemed an appropriate time to end her story for the day. After a short prayer, Marcus thanked Maria for another account of her journey with Jesus. After a brief hug they parted as Marcus returned home. As he walked, he reflected on Maria's accounts of Jesus and his followers, attempting to bring salvation to the people.

Marcus never tired of listening to Maria recount her experiences; he slipped away from his wine business as often as he could. However, he knew the coming autumn grape harvest and wine making would soon limit his visits.

With that in mind, Marcus eagerly returned the next day to the cave to hear more of Maria's story. Maria had reached a painful part of her account, the death of the man she loved and had followed for many months.

Maria proceeded with her account, but she sat at the front edge of her stone seat and her voice was uneven. "When Jesus went to Jerusalem to celebrate Passover at the temple with his disciples, crowds met him and greeted him as the Messiah. Passover was always an exciting time, and his followers were overjoyed, elated by the large, enthusiastic crowds. Celebrating Passover in Jerusalem is an important event for every Jew but to be celebrating with Jesus was even more meaningful for those people who were close to him. We hoped that somehow this festival would lead to the coming of the kingdom that Jesus had promised.

But it did not work out that way at all. The Romans captured Jesus and put him in prison. At the insistence of the Jewish leaders in Jerusalem, the Romans held a mock trial and condemned Jesus to death.

His other close followers and I believed that the Jewish leaders were afraid that the Romans, fearing that Jesus would start a revolt, might punish all Jews. They had good reason to be fearful because the Romans had brutally murdered Jews before. The disciples also suspected that the Jewish leaders thought Jesus a threat to their own high positions."

Maria was only able to give a brief account of Jesus' death because the memory was still painful. "Jesus was crucified, nailed to a cross and left to die. It was a horrible way to die. The disciples and other followers hid or returned to their own cities. Only a few of the women who followed Jesus joined his mother at the cross to witness his death. We held onto each other and wept. We mourned for the end of efforts to bring salvation to the Jews but more important to us at that moment was the loss of someone we greatly loved.

The morning after the Sabbath, three days after the crucifixion, my friend Maria and I went to the tomb to wash and anoint the body of Jesus. When we reached the tomb, the large stone used to seal the entrance was rolled aside and the tomb was empty. Jesus appeared and told me to tell his disciples that he was alive. I ran to tell them of the resurrection, but they refused to believe me. The disciples remained in hiding and many of the other followers scattered. Disappointed and unsure what to do, I returned to my home in Magdala."

Marcus sensed that Maria needed a break after the retelling of this very personal and emotional event. They sat quietly for several minutes before Marcus stood and walked over to Maria. He leaned over and put his hands on her shoulders. She looked up, into his face and he could see tears in her eyes.

"You are such a strong and amazing person," he said quietly. "You experienced such tragedy, loss, and sadness. Yet the sight of Jesus, resurrected, must have brought it all to a moment of relief.

Of course," he continued. "It is only because I know of the spread of Jesus' message and the many people saved that I can feel joy in what you have told me."

Maria stood, thanked Marcus for his support and understanding and agreed that the sadness and the work of spreading the message were all worthwhile.

This time it was Marcus who asked for a prayer of thanks before he departed.

Chapter Five

Maria Begins her Mission

The Gospel in Galilee

Immediately following the death of Jesus, the crucifixion was considered a very bad omen, a sign of finality. It was viewed by many of his followers as a disappointment, if not a defeat. The resurrection was doubted — even by some of Jesus' disciples — and disputed by others. It was certainly not the story the followers of Jesus wanted to emphasize as they tried to win converts.

Despite all Jesus had said to his disciples, some did not fully understand the resurrection. Instead, the disciples continued to preach repentance and the coming of the kingdom of God or they simply remained in hiding, discussing options, and asking questions they could not answer.

As a result of the uncertainty, the followers of Jesus were in disarray. Some of the disciples and other followers left the area around Jerusalem, fearing for their safety. Peter and a small group of apostles remained in Jerusalem, awaiting the return of Jesus and the arrival of the kingdom of God. Those who dared to remain in Jerusalem laid low.

Others, believing Jesus would meet them in Galilee, went there to wait for his return. A few of the followers of Jesus, unsure of the resurrection, returned to their homes and resumed their old occupations. Many of those who had joined the followers of Jesus in his later years had been more curious than devoted and they, too, drifted away.

Because Galilee was far from Jerusalem and the Jewish authorities, those followers who returned there were a bit bolder. Small gatherings, led by one or two disciples, were held secretly in homes in Galilee. Spreading the word about Jesus and the Way was slow and hesitant.

Maria felt the same disappointment as the other followers of Jesus, but she also felt a need to continue spreading his message. She considered what she could do to encourage those who were the most devoted and closest to Jesus.

Maria sensed the fear that inhibited the apostles, the men and women who were important members of the Way. Because they had been publicly associated with Jesus, they were the most sought after by Roman authorities and Jewish leaders. They faced danger in any contact — or even near contact — with representatives of those in power.

Maria shared their feeling of disappointment, fear, and hopelessness. Nevertheless, she felt a special bond, a need, a determination to spread the message of Jesus. She had heard, in the voices of both John the Baptizer and Jesus, the urgency to call all people, especially Jews, to repent, to commit themselves to the concepts of the law. Even gentiles — and pagans — needed to commit to the ten basic principles of Jewish thought.

Jesus had clearly stated that he would return, and the final judgment would happen within the lifetimes of his generation. Thus there was little time remaining and Maria felt she had to spread his message as widely as possible and had to inspire and reinvigorate the disciples, apostles and others affiliated with the movement.

The grape harvest was in, the grapes were pressed, and the juice was fermenting in the vats. With those tasks completed, Marcus was free to visit Maria more often.

He always looked forward to hearing of Maria's experiences with Jesus and his followers and of her travels in Israel. Likewise Maria looked forward to news of Tegulata, the city where she had lived for many years, and many of her friends were there. Time passed quickly as the two friends shared news, joys, and laughs.

Autumn had arrived, the weather was cooler, trees were in full color and crops had been harvested. There was a chill in the air as Marcus once again made his way to Maria's cave. At least the sun was shining, giving promise of a warmer, more pleasant afternoon.

Marcus was eager to hear more of Maria's story and he walked quickly from the city. The rural landscape was still lovely, although many of the colorful leaves now lay, faded, on the ground. Marcus, his body kept fit and agile by the hard labor of his profession, strode briskly along the now familiar trail. Occasionally, a small animal, such as a fox, scurried across the path. In all but the coldest months, many birds were seen and heard in the trees and bushes beside the trail.

Maria had a small fire burning near the entrance to the cave to relieve the morning chill. The temperature deep in the cave was always about fifty-five degrees year-round, moderating the temperature near the entrance. Nevertheless, Maria wore a heavy wool shawl wrapped around her shoulders to ward off the morning chill.

Over the years, Maria had become comfortable in her home in the cave. It provided shelter from the rain, the rare snow, and extremes in temperature from winter cold to summer heat. It was secluded and quiet, perfect for meditation, but not completely isolated from contact with people seeking consolation in times of sadness and distress.

The walls of the cave where she lived were rounded and smooth. Some areas had been smoothed by water flowing through cavities in the rock. Most of the polished surfaces were the result of slow deposition of travertine by the same circulating ground water. The travertine had been laid down slowly, thin layer by thin layer over thousands of years. Some cave formations deep in the cave had strange shapes, as if an abstract artist had created whole new life forms in stone.

The act of sitting on a stone seat, sharing news and memories of earlier lives became a calming ritual. Once Marcus was seated on a large stone in the sun and close to the rock overhang, Maria was ready to proceed with her account.

Marcus began by saying, "Those close to Jesus, as you were, traveled almost constantly and conditions must have often been unpleasant. Nevertheless, traveling with someone as great as Jesus and being among his companions and followers must have been fascinating, even exciting at times.

Maria replied, "There were times when my life with Jesus was more than interesting! There were a few times when I feared for my life and even for the safety of the group of Jesus' followers. Romans were usually tolerant of the Jews but occasionally they could be quite cruel and harsh. It was a dangerous time, and we were always on guard.

People, including some Jewish authorities, occasionally disagreed with Jesus' teachings. Crowds could become agitated and even threatening. Theology and Jewish history are taken very seriously by Jews. Jesus always seemed to sense when things were becoming tense, and he spoke calmly to end the argument.

Like most of the followers of Jesus, especially those in and around Jerusalem, I sometimes feared for my life. Both Roman and Jewish authorities continued to search for followers of Jesus. After a few days I left the city and returned to Magdala. Although I knew Jesus had been resurrected and had appeared to me, to his disciples and to a few others of his followers, I felt a great sadness as I walked north.

Once I settled into my family home in Magdala I returned to my old daily routines. I rejoined my family and friends, happy to be with them again and they were glad to have me home. It was easy to slip back into the daily patterns I had followed for many years. But the desire, the need to spread the message of Jesus was too strong to ignore.

At first I was hesitant to speak to strangers, but I soon found the courage to start a conversation. A large part of my confidence came from my parents. Shopping in the markets with my mother, I saw her unafraid to say what she wanted and why she felt something was not right. She could be quite firm, but I have wonderful memories of her more typical confident, easy-going manner.

When I was with my father in his workshop, he encouraged me to participate in discussions with men in the shop. I mostly listened and learned but sometimes was able to ask a question or even express an opinion. Most men were polite and respectful, listening to what I said, increasing my confidence."

Maria almost laughed when she said, "Jesus, of course, did not need anyone to give him confidence. As Son of God, he came by that attitude quite naturally. But as he was growing up in his father's carpenter shop, he was able to observe people and perhaps benefitted from those experiences.

Jesus always had such insights into people's thinking and attitudes, skills he may have gained from his father, Joseph. Being a successful carpenter in a small town like Nazareth required more than good woodworking skills and a knowledge of construction. One had to be able to deal with people, some of whom could be demanding and unreasonable. Joseph must have been a patient, tolerant man. Jesus certainly encountered many such troublesome people and could deal calmly and patiently with them, often winning them to his side.

Having had such a great teacher and knowing the importance of spreading his message, I set out from my home town. Expecting Jesus to return soon, I felt an urgency to warn as many people as possible."

She sat quietly for several minutes, reflecting on those days of uncertainty and pain.

Finally, Maria continued her story, saying, "When I returned home following the resurrection, I began preaching in the vicinity of Magdala, at first simply speaking to my friends and neighbors in the city. I soon began conversing with local people and with merchants from distant cities. Many men who had known me years earlier were pleased to see me again but surprised I wasn't married."

Maria smiled; a bit embarrassed. She was still charming, attractive, and good company. However, in place of small talk, Maria now talked of Jesus, the coming kingdom of God and the need to repent.

After a brief pause, Maria continued, "I converted many men who were in Magdala on business, and they took with them not only containers of salted fish but knowledge of Jesus and of the Way. As they traveled home, they shared the message of the imminent final judgment and coming kingdom of God with people they encountered.

As I became more confident and found people eager to hear about my experiences as a follower of Jesus, I began to travel farther from my home town. I was usually accompanied by my two close friends, Salome, and Maria. They shared my feeling of urgency to spread the message and were always willing to join me. Having two good friends with me helped, of course."

Maria told Marcus, "I felt safe traveling within Galilee and even north into Syria. It was nice to have companions and someone to share the work and, of course, it was much safer than traveling alone. Our early travels took us north from Magdala to Damascus thence inland to the Jordanian hills. On one occasion we journeyed north and west from Damascus to Antioch and the edge of Asia Minor."

Maria said, "As we entered a new town, we found it easy to converse with groups of women in market places and around village wells. Women, merchants, and others who gathered in markets and central city squares were curious about where we were from, why we were there and about the Way. Some people had heard about Jesus, his preaching, and his miracles, so it was easy to begin a conversation.

The men who followed Jesus, especially the twelve disciples, feared the Roman and Jewish authorizes and were afraid to preach openly. My friends and I, being women, could discuss the teachings of Jesus with little fear of anyone noticing. We were simply viewed as gossiping women. Sometimes we met women by the river or lake shore as they were washing clothes. There we could even baptize people without raising suspicion. Some women brought their husbands to be baptized.

I baptized new followers of the Way as I had been baptized by John. My baptism by John had such a profound impact on me that I had considered myself one of his followers. So did my friends, Salome and Maria, even though we only heard John preach a few times. Thus I wanted to share this moment, this feeling, with those I brought to the Way of Jesus.

She paused, recalling that emotional experience, then said to Marcus, "I hope you don't mind my digression into my personal feelings. But this was my life calling, what inspired me to share the call to repentance and forgiveness preached by John and Jesus."

Marcus replied. "No, I don't mind at all. Your personal experiences, your willingness to share, are part of what made you so effective in winning people to the Way, to repent and follow Jesus. I recall my own baptism very well because it was so meaningful to me. I was baptized by Donnadu, Jeanne's husband. Because he was a friend, and not John the Baptizer, my feelings were not as intense as yours but certainly something I will never forget."

Maria continued, "As autumn began, we returned south to Magdala. We established congregations in several towns in Syria before leaving that region. These included a large community of believers in Damascus.

The city of Magdala is widely known in the Roman empire for its salted fish. The fish are soaked in brine and then dried. The fish, preserved by the salt, last a long time and travel well. The flavor is popular among people in many countries and cultures, so the production and sale of the fish provided a good livelihood for many local people.

Merchants from many places come to Magdala and pay large prices for this highly prized product. Large quantities of salted fish are taken overland to ports on the Mediterranean and shipped to Roman cities around the sea. The presence of travelers from many distant places made Magdala a fascinating place to live.

As a result of this trade, I had contact with many people from far-flung places, far from Magdala, far from Galilee. Thus I was able to spread knowledge of Jesus and the Way to people in many distant places. Before coming here I learned there were communities of followers of the Way in coastal cities in Egypt.

Earlier, my friends Salome and Maria and I learned that, as a result of our preaching to sailors and merchants in Magdala and western Galilee, there are followers of Jesus as far west as Rome.

Because I had been so close to Jesus during his ministry, I felt I had a special role to play. So I felt very good about our success. Through our contacts with sailors and merchants, God provided a way for us to spread the message over a large area without traveling to these distant places ourselves."

Maria's message was simple but emphatic: "Repent! The final judgment is imminent! The kingdom of God is at hand!" Jesus, like John before him, often spoke about the coming kingdom of God and the final judgment. He said it would come within the lifetime of his generation. This left little time to save everyone she encountered. He had warned that no one could predict the day of its arrival; it would come like a thief in the night. He warned people that they needed to be prepared; they must repent and seek salvation.

Within a few years following the resurrection, Maria created a growing group of followers of her own. She preached the resurrection and salvation and told stories of the mission of Jesus as only a close friend and devoted follower could. As a result of this personal connection, she found it easy to win converts.

Although Maria softened her message with personal stories of her time with Jesus and her own life experiences, it was still a somewhat threatening message. Her arguments for salvation were persuasive — and at times insistent — and she convinced many to follow the Way and join the community of believers. Maria, like John the Baptizer and Jesus, warned people of the imminent end of the world as they knew it.

Maria, having been a follower of John the Baptizer, urged people to repent and, as a sign of their change of attitude, be baptized. She believed her baptism with water, like that of John's, would be followed by baptism of the Holy Spirit.

Maria said, "Perhaps now would be a good time to relate what the other followers of Jesus were doing. I should also tell you about some other events in Galilee that greatly affected the followers of Jesus.

"The Jews had long hoped such a person would be sent by God to end the oppression of the Jews. The ancient prophets had described such a person in various ways during the previous thousand years but in each case this Messiah was to free the Jews.

During this time, several men in Galilee had proclaimed themselves to be the Jewish messiah. The first had appeared even before John the Baptizer began preaching along the Jordan and the last one long after the crucifixion of Jesus.

These men claimed they were sent by God to overthrow the Romans. They gathered followers, armed themselves and prepared to fight the Romans. They believed that even though they were greatly outnumbered, God would help them win. But the Romans were much too strong, well-armed and organized. They easily defeated the Galileans and slaughtered many of them.

As word of these false messiahs spread, people were confused and distressed. Some, perhaps many of those, Jesus and his followers had converted, became discouraged and disillusioned after the crucifixion. They lost interest in winning more converts and so the spread of Jesus' warnings of the coming kingdom was slow.

The Romans remained alert to Jews who might attempt a rebellion. To the contrary, the followers of Jesus sought a peaceful kingdom and had no intention of going to war against the Romans. Having seen the brutal Roman response to such rebellions, Jesus' followers avoided attracting attention and suspicions from the Roman — and Jewish — authorities.

The result was that some followers simply returned home to their families and resumed the professions they had before becoming a follower of Jesus. Others limited their efforts to win converts, quietly awaiting the return of Jesus and the arrival of the promised kingdom of God. But one could hardly blame them; it was a dangerous time.

It made me all the more determined to spread the message as far as possible, in Galilee and beyond, to as many people as possible. I felt I needed to speak not only to Jews but to Romans, Greeks, Samaritans, to everyone. Because I had seen Jesus after he was raised, I was possibly more inspired than many of the others. I felt I had to call as many people as possible to repent because the final judgment might occur any day.

But not everyone was discouraged. Some of those who returned home continued to share their experiences and beliefs with family, friends, and neighbors. They convinced many of them to repent and believe in Jesus' message of the coming judgment. And not all left Jerusalem.

Following the crucifixion, some of the disciples and other followers did as Jesus had instructed them. They sold everything they had and formed a small community in Jerusalem. Because they believed Jesus would return soon, bringing with him the kingdom of God, they thought the money they received would be sufficient to support themselves until that happened.

James, Jesus' brother, led the group in Jerusalem, organizing the followers, arranging places to stay, buying food and supplies. When Jesus was alive, Judas had managed the purse. In addition to betraying Jesus, Judas had stolen from the disciples' money. On the contrary, James had a reputation for honesty and treating everyone justly. The followers of Jesus not only trusted James with their money, but they also allowed him to make many decisions regarding the organization and activities of the group.

Peter also remained with this group and usually was the spokesman, leading efforts to gain more followers to the Way. Peter's message was that of Jesus and John the Baptizer: 'repent for the judgment and end of the age was at hand'.

Some other disciples, recalling Jesus saying he would go before them to Galilee, went there to wait for his return. Like those in Jerusalem, they sold everything they had and formed small communities near Capernaum. They, too, anxiously awaited Jesus' return."

Maria paused before saying, "I have talked for a long while. I suddenly realize that I am hungry; perhaps this would be a good time to share the bread you brought."

Marcus broke off pieces of the bread and gave one to Maria. She took it, closed her eyes briefly and ate it thoughtfully.

She slid off the ledge where she had been sitting and said, "I'll be back in just a minute." She disappeared into the cave and returned with two small ceramic cups and a container of wine. As she poured a small amount of wine into each cup, she said "As we recall Jesus and his mission, we should remember his last meal with his disciples."

She handed one of the cups to Marcus before returning to her seat on the rock ledge. She held her cup and looked at it wistfully before sipping slowly. All the while she thought of the many times she had eaten with Jesus and his closest followers. Her dark eyes became moist. It took several minutes for her to resume her emotional presence in Gaul.

After the brief meal, Maria continued her account of her mission, "It was a time of stress for the followers of Jesus. This continued for years prior to my coming here.

But I am getting ahead of myself. During the winter following the resurrection of Jesus I preached mostly in the region near Magdala and west toward the Mediterranean coast. Many of the people I spoke to were merchants and people connected to the sea. When the weather was unsuitable for sailing, sailors and merchants remained in ports for days, sometimes even weeks at a time. They had a lot of time on their hands and enjoyed conversations about a new religion. I was able to talk to them for long periods, teaching them about Jesus, his preaching, works and healing the sick, the blind and others.

It was difficult because many people I encountered had been raised with strong beliefs unlike ours. Because they came from foreign lands, many were pagans believing in multiple gods. I enjoyed the challenge, convincing them their gods were powerless and that my God, our God, is all powerful and Jesus is our connection with him. Many people were convinced and were willing to change their beliefs, their behavior and become followers of the Way."

Maria paused before continuing, "Sometimes it was difficult but even Jesus faced difficulties. I saw that many times. Jesus encountered opposition, especially from strict Jews. However, he was very wise and could defeat challenges from both Jews who denied his message and from Roman pagans who did not want to give up their own gods.

Like all devout Jews, as a youth and young man, Jesus had listened carefully to the rabbis in the synagogue. He knew much of the Jewish scriptures by heart, and he had a keen understanding of the truth behind the ancient scriptures."

Maria said, "Many times I was amazed at how Jesus could confound Jews who confronted him. Even very learned Jews could not win an argument with him. Those around Jesus were always astounded by his knowledge and wisdom.

I was delighted to share Jesus' teachings and his love for all people. He attracted, even sought out, the poor, the sinners, the outcasts, those with illnesses, diseases, and physical disabilities — the blind, the lame, lepers, and many people possessed with demons. Some he healed, others he encouraged and gave them hope of a better life in the kingdom to come.

The converts returned to their home towns, and even further, to their home countries, and spread the knowledge of God, Jesus, and the Holy Spirit. They shared the message of the kingdom of God and the coming judgment with many other people over a large area. Maria's message was spread as far as Italy and Egypt, and communities of believers grew in many towns and cities there. As a result, congregations, which later became organized churches, were established in many distant cities."

Maria confided to Marcus, "I would love to have traveled to Rome or Egypt, to teach in those distant communities. However, I had no way to travel that far, and it wasn't safe for a woman to travel alone. Even three women traveling together were not always safe. It is especially dangerous in cities along the sea. A woman alone there would be considered a prostitute and treated as such. So I had to be content simply knowing those communities of followers of the Way we inspired had spread so far.

In my own conversations with people here in Gaul, I stressed that Jesus had urged charity, generosity, kindness and compassion. Many times he said, 'Do unto others as you would have them do unto you. And likewise, do not do to others as you would not have them do to you.'

When Maria was a missionary in Israel and even Syria, many of the people that she encountered had heard about Jesus. They were either Jews or were familiar with Jewish beliefs. In Gaul no one had heard of Jesus, and most were not familiar with Judaism and Jewish scriptures. Maria was very knowledgeable because her father, in addition to arranging lessons in Latin, had taught her about Jewish beliefs and the scriptures. Even though she was a girl, he wanted her to be familiar with Jewish traditions and history.

When talking with Gauls, Maria had to begin with the very basics. She had to explain monotheism and the idea of heaven. Only then could she talk about salvation and the coming final judgment.

Marcus was impressed with all of the events and activities Maria had described. He was impressed with what Jesus and his small band of followers had done. He was amazed that one person, with a small group of uneducated followers, could have such an impact and inspire such devoted followers.

Maria spoke of her personal experiences with Jesus, such as being present when he fed a large crowd, hundreds of people, with just a few fish and several loaves of bread. She told of more intimate times, such as sitting around a fire with the disciples, listening and asking questions. It was often these personal stories that had touched listeners gathered around Maria and convinced them that she told the truth.

She told of the many healings Jesus accomplished. She, too, healed, but less dramatically, usually using medicinal herbs. In her contacts with women, both in Galilee and in Gaul, Maria observed the use of plants to heal wounds and cure illnesses. These traditional treatments had been passed down for many generations and had proved to be effective. Maria also brought emotional healing to others simply through her calming words and understanding of people's needs and hurts. It was the many stories and kind acts Maria shared that led many to the Way.

Maria said, "Jesus often taught using parables, short stories with obvious truth on the surface but whose meaning, whose relation to his message of salvation, was often hidden. He had a great knowledge of language, often using an unexpected word or phrase. Sometimes he used a play on words or a phrase from scripture to make a point. It was a pleasure just to listen to him. I tried hard to understand and learn from everything he said."

Maria used some of Jesus' parables, including the mustard seed and leaven, tailoring them to her audience of Gauls and Romans. The parable of the farmer sowing seeds, some falling on stones or shallow soil, while some thrived, was a natural among rural people in Gaul.

"Just as Jesus often had to explain the parables to his listeners, I had to interpret them to my listeners. I had to choose parables that could be understood, at least on the surface, by the people here. Some stories Jesus told would only make sense, even superficially, to people in Israel, some only to Jews. Stories about Jewish laws prohibiting work on the Sabbath would puzzle even Romans living here."

Maria's approach to relating to people, to telling them of Jesus, was very personal. In addition to telling of her close relationship with Jesus, she drew on her own life story. Her success was in part due to her personality which was outgoing, lively, positive, and caring. Just as she had been a delightful, charming, spirited young woman growing up in Magdala, she continued these qualities as an adult. Her encouragement, especially of women, put people at ease. Her attitude was both outgoing and easy-going which reduced people's tensions and allayed their concerns. Like Jesus, she welcomed children, the poor, the weak and the discouraged.

Marcus listened intently as Maria spoke, attentive to the details and insights in the accounts of her life. There was a pause and he asked, "Was anyone else who had known Jesus spreading Jesus' story so far from Galilee, converting people in distant places to the

Way? What about the disciples and others who had followed Jesus? You said that they remained in Jerusalem or Galilee."

Maria replied, "As I said earlier, most of the disciples retuned to Galilee, mostly around the Sea of Galilee, explaining the teachings of Jesus to the Jews. Some remained in Jerusalem, spreading the gospel there, also mostly to the Jews. The disciples considered that bringing salvation to the Jews had been Jesus' real goal. They believed that followers of Jesus must live according to Jewish laws and traditions. That was the attitude of the group in Jerusalem, led by James, brother of Jesus. They were, in fact, quite adamant about that.

The disciples were, of course, Jews, and nearly all of those Jesus had converted were Jews. So, for the disciples it made sense to preach to Jews. However, Jesus had converted several people who were not Jews and he told us to go to all the world, preaching his message. Knowing this, I preached to any who would listen: Jews, Romans, Greeks, and Syrians. I believed that they all must repent before the judgment of God came to all people."

After the crucifixion, followers of Jesus were under pressure from both the Romans and the Jewish authorities. The Romans considered them potential revolutionaries. The Roman authorities were not sure what was meant by the imminent coming of the kingdom of God, but saw it as a threat to Roman rule. The people of Galilee in particular had always been troublesome, threatening to overthrow Roman rule. Romans were thus suspicious if not fearful of the talk of a new kingdom of any sort.

To add to the tension, Jewish leaders did not believe Jesus had been the promised Messiah. As far as they were concerned, he had been one of several failed claimants in times past. They thought the claims of Jesus' resurrection to be at best nonsense and certainly blasphemy.

The disciples tried to discuss the coming kingdom of God and Jesus' resurrection in the synagogues, but they were quickly thrown out. Ultimately James, the brother of Jesus and leader of those in Jerusalem, was killed, thrown off a cliff by the leading Jews. Teaching about the Way was driven underground in Judea. It fared only slightly better in Galilee.

Roman authorities continued to be concerned about Jews, knowing they resented the Roman occupation and harbored hopes of overthrowing the Romans. Now, with the added tensions about Jesus, the Romans especially feared the Jews might attempt a revolt. The disturbances surrounding the final days of Jesus were fresh in their memories.

As Maria traveled around Galilee she frequently saw small groups of Roman soldiers loitering in markets and other gathering places. More than just keeping eyes on Jews, they inquired about followers of Jesus, suspecting them to be likely trouble makers.

Maria was glad the Romans only sought male followers of Jesus, believing women too weak or too docile to be a problem. Although Roman women were permitted education and some freedoms, Roman men could not believe Jewish women had similar freedoms. Romans could not imagine Jewish women having the freedom to speak out, to convince men to believe in some new kingdom.

Maria paused, thinking of the many attacks on those followers who preached the word of Jesus. Although many people came to hear her and others calling for repentance and an end to sin, there was still great opposition to her message.

Then she continued, "I later learned that a man named Paul was preaching a message much like my own in Asia Minor, even to congregations I had established there. Because it was difficult for me and my friends to travel so far to revisit these distant communities, we withdrew into Galilee. And it was only a short time before I came here."

I'm not sure when Paul had his vision or began preaching. From what I learned, he only started preaching in Galilee and north of there, where I had preached, nine or ten years after I started, after the resurrection. He also began by preaching south of Judea, in Arabia, for three years. He did not want to work in places where Jesus was already known, duplicating work of others. I suspect he also wanted to avoid places where he had persecuted Christians earlier. He had begun using his Greek name, Paul, instead of his Jewish name, Saul, so people would not immediately make the connection."

Maria continued, "I came to Gaul after Paul began preaching in Galilee, Syria, and Asia Minor. While I knew little of Paul's message, I didn't disapprove because what I did know sounded correct. I also knew that he had never heard Jesus teach but had learned of his saving message in a vision. In a way, this was ironic. Some people were displeased with me for having visions — they said I was possessed with demons — but they easily accepted Paul's accounts of visions."

Maria added, "I believed in Paul's visions because they were so much like my own. It was clear that it was the same spirit that spoke to both of us.

Of course, I had an advantage over Paul. Because I had traveled with Jesus and been so close to him, I could share personal stories about Jesus that Paul could not, stories he did not know. This advantage helped me to win many converts. But I had no problem with Paul aiding and encouraging members of assemblies I had started.

One thing I admired about Paul was that he permitted women to participate in his ministry, as I did. Of course, both of us were simply following the example of Jesus who had many women among his followers."

Once again Marcus asked Maria how she had come so far and why she had chosen to bring the gospel to Gaul.

"It is a long story," Maria sighed. "It wasn't planned. Salome, Maria, and I were kidnapped and forced into a rotting boat abandoned on the Mediterranean shore. Peter's men pushed the boat, with us in it, into the sea. Well, it is a long story. It will have to wait until next time."

Memories of the abduction and being set adrift on the Mediterranean Sea in a stinking, sinking old boat became too much for Maria. Even after all these years, the memories were disturbing. She asked if she could stop there, but she promised to continue the next day. Marcus did not want to stop. The story was so impossible, so unbelievable. At least he knew Maria and her friends survived and somehow reached the shore near Massilia. Reluctantly he agreed and, after a brief prayer, set out for home.

To truly understand Maria's journey to Gaul, one must know of events that took place in Jerusalem. These were events Maria did not know about.

Chapter Six

The Emergence of Paul

Although not part of the story of Mary Magdalene, Paul and his teachings about Jesus crossed paths with Mary's account of Jesus. Because of the parallels and differences between the two versions, it is worth noting Paul, his history and preaching.

Saul was a devout and devoted Jew from Tarsus, in eastern Asia Minor. He was intelligent and, by his own account, well-educated. He claimed to have studied under one of the leading Jewish teachers of his time. Like many Jews of the Diaspora, those not living in Judea or Galilee, he was Hellenized, or influenced by Greek thought and philosophy.

Despite his excellent upbringing, Saul did not consider his status special. He was a short man, quite unimpressive in appearance. He was a tent maker by profession. Tents were widely used and always in demand, so work was easy to find. The tools of the trade were small and easily portable so Saul could ply his trade anywhere he went. An inquisitive person,

Saul enjoyed travel, meeting new people, and learning about their customs.

As followers of Jesus began to seek converts in synagogues, most Jews thought their claims about Jesus were exaggerated and considered the belief that Jesus was the messiah offensive. The Jews found Jesus' followers annoying and tried to avoid or ignore them. Failing that, they simply tolerated them.

Saul, on the other hand, found the views of the heretics more than annoying. He strongly objected to their teachings and actively sought to persecute them. As he traveled around Judea, he spoke stridently of their beliefs, denouncing followers of Jesus as blasphemers and advocating physical attacks on them, even the stoning of popular leaders.

However, while on his way to Damascus to persecute a group of followers of the Way, as they were known, Saul was suddenly struck blind. He heard a voice, which claimed to be that of Jesus, unhappy with Saul's persecution of his followers. Saul was amazed, and terrified, that Jesus had sought him out and spoke to him personally. Saul crumpled to the ground in fear as Jesus, his voice emanating from the air and light surrounding him, denounced his persecution of the followers of the Way.

Saul was taken by his companions into the city where he was treated and cared for by the very people he had come to attack. Troubled by his vision on the road, Saul listened intently to his hosts' conversations about Jesus. Convinced by their kindness, compassion and preaching about Jesus, Saul became a believer in Jesus and his message of salvation.

After being converted, Saul set out to preach this new found conviction. He also shared the story of his miraculous conversion with members of the existing congregations. Not all of his hearers were convinced of his sincerity, however. Listeners were often quite suspicious of his motives and his claim to be an apostle was disputed. The fact that many people remembered his previous persecution of followers of Jesus did not help.

As Saul set out to preach in Judea and Galilee, he encountered many Jews who had met Jesus, who had heard him speak or at least knew someone who had. Saul, on the other hand, knew nothing of Jesus except what he heard during the encounter on the road to Damascus. Even while recovering in Damascus, living with followers of Jesus, Saul showed no interest in hearing stories about Jesus the person or his teachings. Saul later admitted, even seemed to take pride in knowing nothing about Jesus.

This lack of personal knowledge put Saul at a great disadvantage, and he had very little success winning followers.

Discouraged, Saul traveled south, into Arabia where he developed his message, his interpretation, and his vision of what it meant to be a follower of Jesus. As a thoughtful, educated and Hellenized Jew, he was influenced by his knowledge of history and Greek philosophy.

Saul had another reason to go to Arabia. He had witnessed the stoning of Stephen; he had even encouraged the stoning. The image of Stephen's death haunted him. It was in his dreams, it awakened him at night. So Saul went to Arabia, into the desert, to meditate, to try to calm his demons.

Even much later, Saul could not rest easy. He remembered his earlier persecution of Christians. He collected money from new converts and took it to Jerusalem. He hoped it would help atone for his earlier crimes.

In the region of Nabataea, also known as Arabia, Saul probably visited cities such as Petra, an important stop on major caravan routes. There he would have encountered travelers from many lands which further increased his knowledge of people and foreign customs and beliefs.

After three years, Saul returned to Damascus. It was then nearly a decade since the crucifixion of Jesus. By now his reputation as a persecutor of Jesus followers was fading. Also during his years in Arabia he used his Greek name, Paul.

From Damascus, Paul began preaching in Galilee, testing his new message. He continued to preach the core message of Jesus: 'Repent, the kingdom of God and final judgment are imminent'. Paul's primary addition to this doctrine was that people were saved by faith, not works. His emphasis was on belief in Jesus and that his death and resurrection ensured believers' entry into the kingdom of God.

As Paul traveled around Galilee, he found existing congregations of followers of the Way participating in a service commemorating Jesus' last supper. Some congregations simply broke and shared bread with a glass of wine while other groups celebrated with a full meal.

Because followers came from all walks of life, some wealthy members brought ample food for themselves while others had little food, often only bread. The wealthy sat with their friends at one end of the table, while the poor sat at the far end. In several instances the meal degenerated into drunkenness because participants drank wine to excess.

In order to eliminate the disparity in how much food each person had and, more importantly, put an end to excessive drinking, Paul sought to restore the commemoration to its original form. He took the breaking of bread and serving a small glass of wine and shaped them into a ritual. He codified the service with a short statement, declaring the bread to symbolize the crucified body of Jesus and the wine his blood.

Paul tied this new ritual to his emphasis on the resurrection of Jesus as a key to salvation. He taught that such knowledge and belief would enable the elect to follow Jesus' ascension into the kingdom of God.

Following the instructions given to him in visions, Paul preached first to Jews but also sought followers among Gentiles. He also welcomed women into his ministry. He was opposed by the leadership in Jerusalem on both counts.

Paul expanded his travels in Galilee and Syria, preaching not only to Jews but also Gentiles, Greeks, and Romans. As he traveled, he not only encountered many people who had heard Jesus or his disciples, but many followers who had been converted by a woman from Magdala, a small city on the western shore of the Sea of Galilee. People spoke of this Maria with enthusiasm, admiration, and reverence. She was said to be an inspiring speaker, someone who was a devoted follower of Jesus, who travelled with him and supported him and his disciples financially. It seemed she had traveled widely in the region, converting many people and assembling small congregations of believers in many places.

Paul quickly decided to take his mission to places not already visited by this impressive and successful woman. He left Antioch and sailed west to the island of Cyprus. He was pleased to find no evidence that Maria the Magdalene had been there.

Chapter Seven

Disagreement Among the Disciples

Andrew could tell when his brother was angry or upset, even when Peter's irritation did not show outwardly. This was one of those times. Andrew took Simon Peter by the arm and asked him to sit with him in the shade of a large oak tree. Andrew made small talk for a while, hoping his brother would relax. He rambled for some minutes before asking Simon what was on his mind.

Simon Peter was indeed upset. He exclaimed, "How dare they pass me over for this leadership position!" He just sat there, fuming.

Despite what Jesus had said about Peter 'having the keys to heaven' and having great authority, James had been made leader of the Jesus movement in Jerusalem. It had been an informal decision by the disciples but a majority decision, nevertheless.

Andrew put his hand on Peter's shoulder and could feel the tension in his muscles. After a pause, he pointed out that James largely remained out of sight, making arrangements, overseeing finances, directing the efforts of the apostles.

Andrew, trying to be positive, said, "While James is arranging lodging, buying food and sending messengers to distant cities, you are traveling around Jerusalem, spreading the message of Jesus, converting many Jews to the Way. You and James have different roles to play, both are important, but yours is more public. You should be pleased because more people, certainly more of the followers of the Way, know your name. Your time will come. Jesus promised you, me, and the other disciples the power to judge people on the day of judgment."

Peter was not pleased at all. He stood up and glared at Andrew, started to say something but thought better of it and walked away, muttering to himself.

Although he would never say anything, Andrew was aware that James, the brother of Jesus, had his own issues. For years, during Jesus' ministry, James and his siblings had doubts about Jesus and his preaching. Jesus' mother and brothers had questioned his wisdom when he disputed the leadership of the synagogue. They were even concerned for his safety. This and his constant absence from home and his failure to fulfill his duties as eldest son also estranged his family from him.

What was almost the last straw occurred once when his family traveled to Capernaum to see him. As they waited outside the house where Jesus was teaching his followers, word was sent to him that they wanted to see him. Jesus said that they were not his family, his followers were his family. That really hurt.

The resurrection had changed James' attitude toward Jesus and now he was a devoted follower. He joined the disciples in spreading Jesus' message of repentance and salvation. James was able to mediate disagreements and disputes among followers. He was such a successful leader and organizer that he became the leader of the congregation in Jerusalem.

With persecution increasing, Andrew left Jerusalem and returned home. As he sat with friends at a rustic table under a grape arbor, relaxing after dinner at the small restaurant, his friend Timothy approached. Andrew stood, greeted Timothy warmly with a big hug.

Timothy quickly asked, "How have you been? What have you done since I last saw you? It has been more than a year. How is your brother, Simon?"

Andrew motioned for him to sit and join the others. "So many questions, so much to tell. You must sit with us."

Once Timothy had greeted the others and settled on the rough wooden bench, Andrew related, in general terms, his life with Jesus and the disciples, the struggles with the efforts to spread the word of the coming kingdom and the successes they had made.

Timothy listened intently, expressing pleasure at the acceptance of Jesus' message and concern for the persecution by the Romans and Jewish authorities.

When Andrew reached a stopping point, Timothy asked, "And what of Simon? What were the other disciples like and how did such a diverse group get along with each other?"

Andrew replied, "For the most part, everyone gets along well. Everyone is so devoted to Jesus and his message, personal differences seldom interfered. I hate to say it, but Simon was the most stubborn, outspoken and pugnacious. If anyone was going to make a scene, it was Simon Peter. Some of the others had concerns, differences, but they kept them to themselves.

"Most of us came from the same background, similar families and experiences. It is easy to relate to each other. We all wanted our people to rule themselves once again. Although it was never talked about, I think we all hoped that the promised kingdom of God meant the end of Roman rule over the Jews."

Over the course of Jesus' ministry, Peter confided many things to his brother. He talked of his hope for an important place in the coming kingdom of God, but he also expressed his doubts and hesitations. Peter sometimes grumbled about his fellow disciples and others who traveled with them. One of these followers in particular, Peter thought had been much too close to Jesus. Her name was Maria Magdalene.

Timothy asked, "When I talked to you earlier, you mentioned women taking part in the group. Did they remain with the group and were there any problems with them?"

Andrew smiled and replied, "A few women continued with us, two or three are with us all the time. There were a few problems. And, of course, most of the problems were Simon Peter's."

Timothy interrupted and said quietly, "Yes, good old Simon. That sounds like him. But were there problems because of them, the women? Was there talk…"

Andrew continued, "One woman especially got on Simon's nerves. She was very smart, very devoted and had money to donate toward our expenses. She was Maria, from the village of Magdala. Simon thought she spent too much time close to Jesus and that Jesus liked her much too much. Jesus did admire her very much because of her devotion and her deep understanding of his teachings."

Andrew took a sip of his wine and continued, "To make matters worse for Simon, Maria Magdalene is now gaining converts and followers all over Galilee. In fact, her fame is spreading beyond Palestine. There are reports she has followers as far north as Syria and as far south as Egypt. Her success adds to Peter's worries and really irritates him."

Andrew confided, "Simon is not completely alone. Some of the other disciples have also been hearing accounts of Maria's preaching in Galilee. She is very successful, winning many converts to the Way. The disciples have no problem with much of what Maria is saying. However, there are reports that she is preaching to Romans, Greeks, and other foreigners as well as to Jews. The disciples can't openly object to that because Jesus had instructed us to go to the ends of the world, to all people, preaching and teaching. However, most still believed we should preach to the Jews first.

"One aspect Maria's efforts that does concern the disciples was that she was not requiring Gentile converts to follow Jewish regulations of dietary practices and men were not required to be circumcised. This had been discussed often among those who stayed in Jerusalem."

As Jews — and Jesus was a Jew — the disciples believed that following Jewish law was necessary to be a follower of Jesus. Nearly all of the followers in Israel thought of themselves as devout Jews.

Timothy finished his wine and thanked Andrew for bringing him up to date on progress of the followers of Jesus.

Timothy gave Andrew a great hug and said, "I hope we'll meet again soon, and you can share more stories of your travels. Give my regards to Simon. And let me know what happens to this Maria from Magdala. I suspect she will go far."

Neither Timothy nor Andrew knew just how far Maria Magdalene would go.

Peter, more than the others, thought about Maria Magdalene and her divergent beliefs. He thought of a way to eliminate some of Maria's followers. Peter sent word, discretely of course, to the Jewish leadership and suggested that Saul, a well-known persecutor of Christians, be sent into Syria to hunt down Christians, most of whom were followers of Maria Magdalene.

When Andrew learned of Peter's plan to attack fellow followers of the Way, he was horrified and angry. He sought out Peter, gave him a good verbal lashing and ordered Peter to have Saul brought back. Peter simply stomped off.

Unfortunately for Peter, somewhere on the way to Damascus, Saul was stuck blind and was healed by followers of the Way, converted and took up Jesus' message. To make matters worse, Paul's message was very similar to that of Maria Magdalene. Now Peter had another challenge to his ego, another competitor for converts. As it turned out, someone else was not insisting converts follow Jewish requirements.

James, as the leader of the congregation in Jerusalem, chose a less drastic solution to Maria's different approach. In an attempt to resolve this issue, he summoned Maria to meet with him and the other disciples. Unlike Peter, James was not opposed to

Maria Magdalene or to other women participating in missionary activities. He viewed her teachings as unorthodox, perhaps a little too personal and intimate. James was known as 'James the Just', and his tolerance of Maria fit that image.

Andrew also had no problem with women taking part in the effort to bring others into the Way. Maria was popular and successful; those she converted were sincere and devout. Andrew was eager to see Maria again and to hear her defense.

When the request from James reached her, Maria was happy to meet with him and the other disciples. After all, they were all followers of Jesus; they had traveled together for several years. The following week she traveled from Magdala to Jerusalem where she met with James and several of the disciples in the home of a follower of the Way.

They met in a room at the rear of the house. The open door and windows admitted a cooling breeze. They sat around a table, rough from years of use for a variety of tasks. It began as a relaxed meeting of old friends.

Maria explained to James and a group of disciples that she was simply teaching what Jesus taught. Jesus talked of the coming kingdom of God, the need for repentance and salvation through faith and repentance. Maria reminded them that she had traveled with them, that she had been a devoted follower of Jesus and listened closely to his teachings.

When asked about Jewish dietary laws, circumcision and other rules, Maria reminded them that Jesus said there should be no rules. He pointed out that Jews were bound by too many laws and restrictions and that his church was not to be legalistic.

Peter sat quietly but fidgeted and was obviously uncomfortable. It wasn't long before Peter began to criticize Maria Magdalene. His dislike for her was obvious. Her success in winning converts and her close bond with Jesus clearly irritated him.

Peter yelled at Maria, "I saw Jesus kiss you... on the mouth! More than once! What else did you do?"

Maria sat quietly.

After a long silence, she said to James, "You had another question about my teachings?"

Peter was about to explode in another outburst, but James held up his hand in Peter's direction. He said to Maria, "You emphasize your closeness to Jesus. You claim a special understanding of Jesus' teachings of the kingdom of God."

Before James could say more, Peter continued, "You claim Jesus told you secret teachings, that you understand things we, his disciples, do not."

Maria pointed out that, in fact, she was a devoted follower who did appear to understand more than most of his followers. Jesus even said so.

Maria said, "As I am sure you remember, Peter, I was with you and the other disciples during much of

Jesus' ministry. I was on the long walks between towns, in the hot sun, the rain and the cold."

Peter interrupted, "Yes, you were always there, sitting close, listening intently, hanging on every word, and asking many questions, too many questions. You were a real nuisance."

Maria took advantage of Peter's need to catch his breath. "Perhaps you should have paid more attention. I have simply been spreading Jesus' message in Galilee and elsewhere, winning many converts to the Way. That is what Jesus told us all to do."

Peter said, loudly, "Yes, we know all that. But because your message and your requirements are not the same as ours, it causes confusion among those joining the Way. And you should go away and leave the preaching to us. Go back to Magdala and stay there!"

Andrew was embarrassed by Peter's continued verbal assault. James and some of the disciples wearied of Peter's outbursts. Even though they did not disagree with Peter at times, they found his hot temper divisive. As leader of the group in Jerusalem, James tried to calm Peter.

Peter, ignoring James' efforts, continued to disparage Maria. He again complained to the other disciples about Jesus' preference for Maria. "He often kissed her on the mouth!" he repeated loudly

Matthew responded, "Yes, he did. But he kissed us all on the mouth. He encouraged us to kiss each other. He said it was symbolic of our sharing his teachings. It shows our love for one another."

Peter was not satisfied. Looking at the other disciples he said, "But when he kissed *her*, it was different. He clearly loved her more than he did us!"

Andrew tried once again to calm Peter. James continued to defend Maria, knowing that she was a devoted follower and Jesus greatly admired her. James suggested she preach to Jews and ignore the issue of rules and regulations because they already followed Jewish law. Maria was not deterred. She planned to continue spreading Jesus' teachings far and wide.

Peter discreetly suggested they keep him informed as to where Maria was preaching.

Chapter Eight

Maria's 'Mission Journey'

Maria did not sleep well. She lay on her bed, a rock ledge covered with a straw mat and a couple of blankets, but her mind would not be still. She thought about the future, the promised coming of the kingdom of God. Jesus had said it would come within the lifetime of those who heard him speak. That included her, but she was growing old. She had no feeling, no intuition that it was imminent.

Maria knew that she had accomplished much, both in Israel and, more recently, in the region she now called home, converting many local people to follow the Way. She knew the movement was well established in southern Gaul, that many people were carrying on her efforts to spread the message of the coming of the kingdom and the need to repent.

Despite these positive thoughts, she knew there were necessary loose ends to tie up, just in case. The uncertainty about how soon the coming of the kingdom of God and Jesus' return would occur troubled her. Gradually a plan came to mind, one without some needed details but sufficiently clear that she finally fell into a restful sleep.

The autumn days became shorter and the weather cooler. The trees and bushes shed their colorful leaves. It was a warm, sunny afternoon when Marcus came again for a visit. On the previous visit, Maria had given the background, as she knew it, of events leading up to her travel westward to Gaul. Marcus was now eager to learn of the journey itself. The idea of her making such a journey seemed unreal. It was miraculous that Maria and her two friends had traveled the length of the Mediterranean Sea, from Israel on the east almost to the Pillars of Hercules on the west. He could hardly imagine that three women, from a small village, traveling alone on such an arduous and risky journey, had survived. His mind was filled with awe, and he had so many questions.

When Maria came out of the cave, Marcus noticed that she seemed to walk a bit slower, and she seemed almost frail. Had he just not noticed it before, or had she changed over the past months? Once she was seated on her usual smooth, flat rock, her eyes sparkled, and she became more animated. Marcus convinced himself she was well.

Maria managed a smile and greeted Marcus. "I am glad that you come so often. A few others come but stay only a short time. It is nice to know they are concerned enough to see that I am well and bring me news and food. When you are here and I can share my message of Jesus, I feel that I am still spreading the warning of the coming of the kingdom of God.

There are times when I wonder when Jesus will return, when God's kingdom will arrive. I thought they would have happened by now. Jesus said these would take place within my lifetime. Perhaps they still will. Even Jesus said only God, his father, knows when the kingdom will arrive, the judgment will take place. We must be patient and wait."

When Marcus and Maria were seated on their stone seats, Marcus said, "I am so amazed with your travels and have many questions. What brought you to Gaul, so far from Galilee, from home, family and your friends and fellow followers of The Way?"

Maria hardly knew where to begin because she did not know herself what prompted the beginning of her journey. It was certainly not her choice. She simply assumed it was part of God's plan.

Maria began her story of travel with her friends Salome and Maria, spreading the words of Jesus in expanding circles from Magdala. She later learned, from Andrew and other disciples that, as time passed, more accounts of her success in winning converts to the Way reached the disciples in Jerusalem.

Maria said, "One day, in a town market not far from Magdala, I encountered Phillip, a close friend, one of the men who had been close to Jesus and his disciples. He told me about the discussions of the disciples in Jerusalem.

"Phillip said the disciples continued to be sought by the Jewish authorities and by the Romans as well. The disciples met with small groups of new converts, mostly in the homes of friends, but they did not dare speak in public or to large groups. They feared that some spy might learn of the meeting places and report them to the Roman or Jewish authorities.

"Nevertheless, they were converting some Jews in Jerusalem. Several of the disciples had returned to the own hometowns and converted many in Galilee as well. They heard from travelers and friends in Galilee that I was also preaching and winning converts."

Although Maria Magdalene had been unaware of it, she was viewed as an important teacher and her message must have had a significant influence far beyond Galilee. As evidence, in the second century, one of her followers in Egypt wrote the 'Gospel of Maria'. Aside from what the content says about her actual teachings, it does indicate that she was believed and revered by many Christians in the Holy Land and Egypt. Other Christian writings of that time expressed admiration of Maria Magdalene in other terms. The texts were copied and widely shared. Fragments of multiple versions have been found.

Maria continued her account of the followers in Jerusalem, "They were pleased to learn that the movement was growing, expanding far beyond Judea and Galilee. However, I also heard that a few of the disciples continued to be displeased that Roman and Greek converts were not being required to follow Jewish laws regarding food, honoring the Sabbath and circumcision. I was told that Peter especially found this news unsettling.

Just as they had called me to Jerusalem to explain and defend my teachings, they also called Paul to Jerusalem. I'm sure I mentioned Paul earlier; he was traveling in Asia Minor, winning converts to the Way with a message much the same as mine. The disciples questioned him as they had me about requiring non-Jews to follow Jewish laws. I don't know how that was resolved with Paul or if it was resolved."

Maria did not know that Peter had decided to get rid of her. He considered simply having her killed, perhaps by faking charges of adultery and having her stoned to death. But by then she had too many followers to risk such an assault. Instead, he decided to 'send her on a mission trip'.

Maria continued, "My two steadfast traveling companions and I slowly worked our way west from Magdala. At first we were nervous about moving to a new town where we didn't know anyone. Gradually, as people accepted us and our message, we overcame our fears. It seemed God had a plan for us.

As we prepared to leave one village, often someone would recommend a relative or friend in the next village who would provide lodging and food. In this way we traveled from village to village, receiving good lodging and enjoying good conversation. Hospitality to strangers is important to everyone in that region. It just comes naturally to us; it is part of our traditions.

Because the three of us primarily traveled on foot, we carried very little. Each had a small bundle of clothes, a small purse for coins plus a cape that protected us from the sun and rain and doubled as a blanket at night.

Hidden within my bundle was the burial cloth from the tomb of Jesus. It was my most precious possession. It was both very personal and very sacred. I kept it close, protecting it with my life. And I believed it would protect my life."

Maria paused, thinking of what came next. Then she continued, "After a month of traveling, meeting new people and winning converts, Salome, the other Maria and I reached the Mediterranean coast. It had been a fascinating, satisfying and successful journey. It had also been long and tiring. We decided to linger near Ptolemais in the home of an absent sailor for a few days. The stay was arranged by a relative of his in the previous town."

The women were unaware that their movements had been observed and their progress reported to certain disciples near Jerusalem. When Peter learned they were near the Mediterranean shore, he set out to accost them.

Maria picked up her account, "Late one evening, as we were washing dishes after eating dinner alone in the house, a group of men appeared in the doorway. I greeted them, identified myself and offered them tea. Once the men were certain we were the women they sought, they ordered us to come with them. They were brusque and offered no explanation; they just gave orders.

We tried to convince them that we were just three women on our way to visit friends in the next town, a village a day's walk along the shore. The men pointed out that we had identified ourselves to them; that the men who sent them had described us in detail. It was clear that we had no defense, and they would proceed with their plans, whatever they were.

We asked if we could gather our few belongings, just our clothes, and they allowed us to do so. One of the men said, 'Yes, get all of your things; we don't want to leave a trace.' Another said, 'Perhaps they will think you ascended into heaven.' They all laughed.

My two companions and I were taken by force to the shore of the Mediterranean. There, our captors found an abandoned hulk of an old fishing boat, stripped of its sail, oars and rudder. I think they thought it probably also leaked, something they considered a plus. Then the three of us, with only our few belongings and little food, were put aboard and the boat pushed into the water. The scruffy old hulk reeked of long-dead fish, rotten seaweed and damp, musty old wood.

When we were forcibly placed into the small ship and set adrift, I hid the burial shroud in my arm load of clothes. I hoped its presence with us would somehow protect us on our journey into the unknown.

The evening breeze, blowing seaward, carried the boat away from land. Soon we encountered a westward current that took us farther from shore, farther from Israel."

At this point, Maria paused for several minutes and then said to Marcus, "I know this is a bad place to stop but the story is too difficult to tell. Remembering this terrible time is too emotional, it brings back too many terrifying memories. If you can come tomorrow, I promise to complete this part of my tale."

Marcus reluctantly agreed. He took Maria's hands in his and said, "I am not certain I will sleep tonight, wondering about what came next. At least I know you and your friends completed the journey here safely. I will return early tomorrow."

Once again they parted with a prayer, thanking God for her safe trip.

Map showing cities Mary Magdalene visited on her way from Galilee to Gaul.

Chapter Nine

The 'Mission Trip' Becomes a True Missionary Journey

As promised, Marcus came early the following day, both eager to hear more about Maria's journey and concerned about her health. He was relieved when she emerged from the cave and into the dappled sunlight. Maria's appearance seemed brighter than the day before and her smile warmer. She looked well and walked easily over the uneven ground. Marcus was relieved to see her both in good health, and good spirits.

Maria greeted Marcus with a hug, pleased to share her story and her faith with him. She selected a place to sit in the warm sun and motioned to Marcus to join her.

She said, "It is another beautiful autumn day, though perhaps a bit cool; I feel much rested and refreshed. I am ready to continue the story of my adventures."

Marcus said, "And I am eager to hear about more this frightening experience. You were about to begin the story of your travel to Gaul. The journey certainly had a frightening start. It is hard to imagine that Peter, a disciple of Jesus, would order such an act. The very thought of being forced into such a decrepit old boat is horrifying.

I hardly slept last night, wondering how you survived, how you came so far, especially in such an unseaworthy vessel. A sea voyage of such a great distance would be tiring, even dangerous, for anyone, and especially for three women. I have heard many sailors tell of sudden storms, ship wrecks, pirates and unpleasant sailors and merchants along the way. Please continue!"

Maria breathed deeply and resumed her account of their travel to Gaul. She said, "Yesterday my story was not very pleasant and the memories of it still troubles me. Now the story will be more cheerful. I feel relaxed and ready to share the rest of my adventure with you."

Maria began, "Soon after being set adrift we realized that at least the rotten old boat didn't leak. We all expressed amazement and considered that our first miracle. A second good sign was the beautiful sunset. The colorful sky with its brilliant reds and oranges brought to mind the saying my father taught me, 'red sky at night, sailor's delight.' A colorful sunset foretold good sailing the next day. With a feeling of assurance, the three of us huddled in the covered bow of the boat and slept.

The morning was calm, but we were out of sight of land. We had no idea how far we had drifted or where we were. More important, we had no idea where we were headed or how we would get there. We prayed for another miracle.

Finally, the first light of dawn brightened the eastern sky. I believed that God had a plan for me and that this event was somehow part of that plan. I continued to believe that the burial shroud of Jesus, still tightly held in my arms, would protect me. I began to make mental plans for what would come next.

We made ourselves as comfortable as possible, lying on the hard wood in the crowded bow. The rocking of the boat, the lapping of the waves against the sides, lulled us to sleep again. A few hours later, the bright morning light ended our sleep."

The morning, pleasant at first, became much warmer as the sun rose higher in the sky. The smell of decaying wood, rotting fish and seaweed combined to form a rather unpleasant odor. Nevertheless, the three women returned to the cramped enclosed space at the bow of the boat to escape the sun, now high overhead. By mid-afternoon, the heat and stench of the boat's past life once again drove them out onto the open part of the boat.

The three women, uncertain of their fate, adrift in the stripped and abandoned old boat, had no doubt that

God had had a purpose for their ordeal. They calmly chatted among themselves, recalling and reflecting on their experiences with Jesus and his followers. They compared observations about the disciples and other serious followers of their teacher. They shared stories of people in the crowds and laughs about unexpected events.

Maria silently reflected on that time of mixed anxiety and hope before continuing, "Thanks to my father's many contacts with ship captains and sailors, I knew of many ports along the north coast of the Mediterranean. I was also aware of the rough life and dangers in coastal cities. However, my father had heard of some distant cities where people were said to be pleasant and at least somewhat welcoming to strangers. The question was, of course, how would get from here to there?"

Memories of her father and childhood caused Maria to pause and gaze into the distance. She also relived in her mind that uncertain morning at sea.

It was several minutes before Maria continued, "We were adrift far off the coast of Galilee when a ship came into view. We waved our cloaks and yelled as loud as we could. Some of the men on the ship heard us and changed course to bring their ship closer. When they saw that we were three women in a decrepit old boat, they sent a small boat to rescue us.

Needless to say, we were immediately barraged by questions from the men in the boat: What were we doing out here? How did we get here? Who were we? While everyone seemed to be talking at once, they rowed us back to the ship.

After being rescued by the Roman merchant ship, my friends and I met the ship's captain. He asked us much the same questions as the sailors: Who we were and how we came to be at sea, so far from shore.

I told him it was a little complicated, that we didn't chose to be at sea. I said that first I should answer his questions in order. I told him that we were from Galilee, followers of Jesus and the Way. I explained that Jesus was the Jewish Messiah and preached that the end of time is near. The Day of Judgment will come soon and so people must repent and sin no more.

The captain said, 'I have heard of a Jew named Jesus; he is said to be a righteous man, perhaps a holy man of some sort. If you are followers of this man, I guess you won't be interested in bedding down with any of the men tonight. They were already casting lots to see which of them would have the first choice of you three. I will put an end to that. I don't know that I will be giving up sin, but I don't want any of my crew adding to their condemnation by molesting one of you. Many sailors believe that just having a woman on board endangers the ship anyway. I can't risk seeing my ship go down because of their bad behavior.'

After a brief pause, the captain asked, 'But why were you so far at sea? How did following this Jesus get you way out here in that boat?'

"I responded, 'Jesus told his followers to spread his message of repentance and salvation to the ends of the Earth.'

Then the captain almost laughed and asked, 'And just where you were hoping to go toward the end of the Earth?'

I said, 'As far west as we could go.' The coast of the Roman province of Gaul in particular seemed to have appealed to my father. He mentioned it to me several times. So I suggested to the captain we would like to go there.

I said to the captain, 'To Gaul. That is almost the end of the Earth. From there our message would spread like ripples expanding from a dropped stone, eventually reaching the end of the Earth.'

The captain laughed. 'To Gaul? The boat you chose hardly seemed up to such a long, arduous journey.'"

Maria said, "My friends and I also laughed. Then I told the captain, 'We didn't choose the boat, it was chosen for us. It was no doubt part of God's plan for us. God works in strange and mysterious ways. Perhaps you and your ship are part of his plan as well.'

The captain said the orders from the ship's owners were to go only to Ephesus and deliver the cargo. If

God wanted him to sail any farther he would have to speak with the owners.

Of course, when we were picked up by the Roman ship, we had no idea where they were going and certainly had no choice in the matter. We were pleased when we learned the destination was Ephesus, on the west coast of Asia Minor. I had heard that it was a beautiful city and quite large.

"We took advantage of the days on the ship to talk with the captain and sailors. In addition to sharing accounts of our lives and experiences, we talked to them of Jesus, the coming kingdom of God and the judgment. The sailors told of their own travels and adventures. We found their stories fascinating and they broadened our knowledge of the world, its diverse inhabitants and their different customs.

When the ship reached port a few days later, the captain remarked on the smooth sailing and quick trip. As we left the ship he told us, 'Perhaps you brought us a blessing from your God. I hope the rest of your journey to Gaul goes as well.'

I told the captain, 'Thank you. I hope your enterprise succeeds. Think of what we have told you about the Way and the coming judgment. Peace be with you and your men.'

When we left the ship, the captain simply pointed us in the direction of the city center and wished us well with our travels. The ship had docked at the long stone and concrete wharf in the port of Ephesus. It was a large structure, and many ships and smaller boats were tied up along its length. Ships came from many ports around the Mediterranean. The multitude of languages spoken by the workmen matched the variety of goods being delivered. We had to walk nearly half the length of the dock to reach the edge of the city."

The docks were crowded with stacks of amphoras, some short, some taller, made of terracotta fired to a dull orange color. They were made by the thousands and shipped by the hundreds, containing wine, olive oil, olives and other items shipped in bulk. Interspersed along the dock were piles of sacks, most filled with grains such as wheat.

The women walked quickly along the wharf, heads up and looking straight ahead. They tried to give the appearance that they had done this before and knew where they were going. They passed many muscular and rough looking men. Fortunately, most were busy moving cargo, and few paused to look in their direction.

After passing several large warehouses between the docks and the city they came to a large, magnificent theater. Sailors on the ship talked about the theater and the Greek and Roman plays performed there. They said it would seat 25,000 people. Maria and her friends paused but decided not to enter and continued toward the city center.

At the theater they turned, following the broad main street whose size and opulence suggested an impressive city ahead. The street was paved with flat stones and marble and lined with a variety of shops, also covered with gleaming marble. They soon came to an ornate marble building, several stories tall. The sailors had told them of this building, exceptional in its size and beauty as well as the collections of books it housed.

Maria picked up her story, "As we stood, awed by the grand architecture, a small dog rushed up to us. It greeted us with its vigorously wagging tail, as if recognizing us as strangers. As I looked down at the dog, I noticed an odd design carved in the marble pavement.

As we stood looking at the strange symbol, an older woman stopped and, in response to our question said, 'It is a notice of a brothel and points in its direction. Disgusting!' She looked at us and said, 'I hope you are not looking for work!' and quickly turned and walked away.

We continued along a wide road paved with marble and lined with shops, shrines and fountains, both decorative and for providing water to residents. Everything was covered with marble that gleamed in the bright sunlight.

"We saw many temples and shrines to numerous pagan deities, both Roman and Greek. It appeared the people here were very devoted to these false gods. We learned later that the local economy depended on the worship of these deities. The sale of votive offerings and incense for household shrines supported many of the local people. We realized we would not convert many residents of Ephesus.

After wandering for a short distance we located the city market. Like the rest of the city, it was large, well laid out and all surfaces were covered in marble. It seemed that shops sold everything one could want, from fresh fruits and vegetables, a variety of meats as well as wine, fabric, ceramic vessels, metal objects of every sort and much more.

We were surprised to find a woman in one shop selling salted fish from Magdala. When we told her we were from there she was excited to meet us and was full of questions. After an extended animated conversation we told her a very brief explanation of how we came to be in Ephesus and asked if she knew somewhere we could stay for a night or two. She was more than happy to offer us a place to sleep as long as we could sleep on a mat on the floor with only a blanket. That was better than we had some nights in Galilee, so we gladly accepted.

She prepared a simple meal when we met her that evening at her home. We met her mother and three children; her husband was traveling, visiting farms to buy fruits for his own business.

In addition to telling our host more about Magdala and salted fish, we also told her of Jesus and the coming kingdom of God and the need to repent. She understood salted fish processing but, as a pagan, had difficulty with the idea of only a single God and salvation provided by God's son who died and was resurrected. Salome, Maria, and I did the best we could to explain it all to her, but it was all too strange for her to understand.

After our experience with our pagan host and our failure to convince her that the kingdom of God was to arrive soon, we felt that staying in Ephesus longer would not be worthwhile. We hoped that we had left a seed with her that might be later watered and sprout and grow. We also hoped that we would have better success elsewhere.

The next day we returned to the harbor to seek a ship sailing west. The waterfront was considerably rougher than the city center and smelled of fish and rotting food, seaweed and worse. We walked along the long dock, looking for suitable ships to take us farther west. We discussed the size and type of each vessel, its condition and cargo and judged the potential for places to sleep. We also tried to observe the appearance of the crew, to get an idea of how they might treat us.

Once we felt a ship would be safe, we sought out the captain or another officer. The first captains we spoke to have no desire to take three women on their ship, regardless of whether they had space or were going where we wanted to go.

After several hours we located a Greek ship captained by a friendly man who beckoned us to come closer. We explained, very briefly, who were and where we wanted to go. He said he sometimes took his sons with him on short trips and even took his young daughter once or twice.

The ship was a little smaller than the one that had rescued us, but we would not be on the open sea this time. He was not going far, just to Corinth, but at least it was going in the proper direction. He said he would be sailing the next morning.

The woman who had hosted us the previous night was pleased to have us stay a second night. Although she thought our beliefs in a single god strange, she enjoyed our talk about Jesus and stories about our lives in a distant foreign place.

We awoke early the next morning and returned to the harbor. We found the ship and were greeted by the captain who seemed quite pleased to see us.

The captain said, 'I have heard rumors among sailors of three women trying to reach the end of the Earth. I assume that is you. The rumors say these women have brought steady winds and a safe voyage to the ship they were on. I hope your god will bless us with such good sailing.'

It was a short journey across the Aegean Sea to Greece. Indeed, we did have good winds and smooth sailing. God continued to bless us and our mission.

When the ship reached to port city of Cenchrea, it docked next to a larger ship already unloading its cargo. Once this ship was reloaded, its next destination was Rome. This was perfect. Not only was it going in the right direction but taking us to an important city.

The two captains talked, and our captain put in a good word for us, relating our smooth journey from Ephesus and the rumors he had heard about us. The next ship would be sailing west in a few days and the captain offered us passage. We were pleased to find another ship so quickly even though it would take several days to unload and load cargo for the next trip.

Rather than stay in the port city, we decided to travel inland to Corinth. I had heard good things about Corinth and was eager to see it for myself. I learned from sailors and merchants stopping in Galilee that Corinth was a pleasant city, and the people were hospitable."

The ancient Greek port of Cenchrea bustled with men loading and unloading ships, wagons and packing animals. The workers were stout and strong, easily, almost gracefully, lifting heavy containers. After years of hard labor they had developed large muscles and strong backs. They were rough and their behavior and language often equally coarse.

As the three women walked away from the docks, they passed two rough looking men sitting idly beside the road. The men's robes were dirty, their long hair matted with grime, as were their unkempt beards. Even though the women passed on the far side of the road, the unpleasant smell of the men was obvious.

As the women passed, the men got up from their perch and began to follow them. The men talked loudly, made threatening comments and laughed at their own crude remarks. They made no secret of their bad intentions.

Maria and her companions walked a bit faster, urging each other along and trying to remain calm. The scruffy men followed, keeping pace with the Maria and her friends whose sense of alarm increased.

Suddenly, as if conjured out of the ground, four Roman soldiers walked out of a doorway, almost colliding with Maria. The soldiers paused, glanced at the women and gave a stern look at the men behind them. The two crude men abruptly turned aside and disappeared from sight, quickly losing interest in the women.

Maria patted the bundle she was carrying, the bundle containing the burial cloth of Jesus.

She quietly said, "I told you it would protect us, that Jesus would protect us." The three smiled and, encouraged, walked lightly over the stone road.

Chapter Ten

The Long Journey Continues

The three women hurried away from the bustling docks and the harbor with its large warehouses, dark, narrow alleys and strong smells. They walked quickly into the city of Cenchrea. As they left the hustle of the port area, they came to an open space at the edge of a residential area. They paused and sat on a low wall to catch their breath and contemplate what to do next.

An old man sat nearby, watching two men loading a horse-drawn wagon. After a few minutes, the man moved closer and greeted the women. Recognizing them as foreigners, he asked what brought them there. Maria Magdalene, always eager to speak with people and spread the word of Jesus, greeted him and began an answer.

The old man, quickly sensing Maria had a story to tell, stopped her and asked, "Is this a long story?"

Maria was caught off guard by the question but the man's expression, almost a smile, suggested he was not simply cutting her off. She replied, "Well, not very long… but not very short either."

He said, "In that case, perhaps you and your friends would like a ride with me on the wagon. That will give you time to finish your story. You can ride as far as you like. I am going to Corinth with these sacks of turnips. It is a much nicer city than Cenchrea and you'll be welcome there."

Maria saw this as another act of God, taking them to the very city they wanted to visit. She quickly agreed and the man helped them into the well-worn old wagon, clearing a place for them to sit among the sacks.

As they traveled slowly along the Roman road, Maria continued to tell of their journey, about Jesus, the coming kingdom of God and the judgment. The old man had many questions but seemed convinced of the coming judgment. He prolonged the discussion of the kingdom of God and the need to repent.

"As we entered the market in Corinth, we thanked the driver, wished him peace and good health. He helped us down from the wagon and wished us well with our continued travels. He said he would think seriously about everything we had told him.

We walked around the market and sought out the synagogue where we hoped to find women who might offer us lodging. Often, we simply went directly to the city market where we could depend on encountering many women. In this case one of the sailors suggested we visit the synagogue as it was the Sabbath, and many people would be gathered there.

As we approached the synagogue, a well-dressed woman came up to us. She greeted us and inquired where we had come from. Our appearance and clothes clearly marked us as foreigners. She introduced herself as Pricilla and said she, too, was not a local. She said she had been a resident of Rome until the emperor had forced some Jews to leave the city. She understood what it was like to be a newcomer and offered us lodging, food and good company. We eagerly agreed to follow her.

Pricilla and her husband, Aquila, welcomed the three of us into their surprisingly large home. Although not really spacious, it was larger than typical, as Pricilla and Aquila had been able to bring some of their belongings from Rome when they left. Now they were looking forward to returning to Rome.

Pricilla told us that when Claudius became emperor, after Gaius was murdered, they were concerned that Claudius might increase attacks on Jews or even order their expulsion from Rome as Tiberius had done. They were told by a friend in the imperial government that the emperor was unhappy with the Jews and was about to begin persecuting them. No one knew what that meant but Romans were not subtle about such things.

Aquila and Pricilla had the money, transportation available and friends in Corinth so they decided to go there. Corinth was a pleasant place to wait and see what would happen in Rome. It turned out the persecution was not serious, and, in fact, they learned that Claudius had sent a letter to authorities in Alexandria, Egypt, urging toleration of Jews. Pricilla said they were never conspicuous among those in Rome, so they felt safe there. With that in mind, they decided to return.

As we walked around the city that afternoon, we encountered a friend of Pricilla's, a woman named Phoebe. We had a long talk about many things, and I briefly mentioned Jesus and our mission to spread his message of the coming kingdom of God. Both Priscilla and Phoebe were curious and interested so I promised I would tell them more after dinner.

During dinner, questions from our hosts allowed me, Salome and Maria to tell them in detail about Jesus and his message of salvation and the coming kingdom of God. There were many more questions and the discussions carried over for several days.

During that time, Pricilla and Aquila were making arrangements to return to Rome. I told them that we had already arranged passage on a ship sailing to Rome. Aquila was familiar with the ship and its captain and said it would provide a safe journey. Aquila was impressed that the captain had agreed to take us — three women — on board. Aquila said we must have quite a good reputation for bringing good weather and suitable winds to obtain such acceptance.

It was agreed that Pricilla and Aquila would join us, Salome and Maria and we would all travel together.

Aquila was able to arrange for him and Pricilla to travel on the same ship with us.

Pricilla had friends who had already returned to Rome, and they were eager to greet their old friends. Pricilla assured us she was certain she could find accommodation for us, her three new friends.

It was only a few days before Aquila had their belongings taken to the harbor in Cenchrea and loaded on the ship we had arranged. Soon we were onboard a large merchant ship and underway. There was ample space for us to be comfortable and have privacy. Once again we enjoyed good weather and calm seas.

On the ship between Cenchrea and Rome we met a young captain in the Roman army. He was being sent by the army to Massilia. Although the region was peaceful, the emperor Claudius wanted a strong military presence there to ensure it stayed that way. During our time at sea we spent many hours talking about our families, travels, and his life in the Roman army. Of course, we also talked about religion; he was a pagan, and we compared his beliefs and ours. He was curious about Judaism, having never actually talked with a Jew. We explained about Jesus and his mission to warn everyone, not just Jews, about the coming final judgment and the kingdom of God. Our journey to Rome took several days, so we had plenty of time to give him much to think about."

Pricilla and Aquila welcomed Maria and her companions into their home in Rome. They had sent word of their planned return from Corinth to friends in Rome who prepared the house for their homecoming. The house was clean; the windows open to allow fresh air to cool the rooms.

"The house was much larger than my home in Magdala. Instead of a few small rooms around a courtyard, there were larger rooms around an atrium and portico. It had several bedrooms and even a separate dining room. My home had stone floors; their home had lovely mosaics with pictures of flowers and animals surrounded with elaborate borders. I was very impressed!

It was late in the day when we arrived at Pricilla and Aquila's home. Their daughter was recently married; her now empty bedroom was large enough for the three of us. It was decided they would stay there that night. That evening, Pricilla invited her daughter Cecilia to join us for dinner. She lingered for hours, discussing our lives and families.

As we shared accounts of growing up, Cecilia asked me if I had ever been married. I responded, almost with a laugh, 'No, my situation was, well, a bit different. You and your parents are fortunate.' I looked at Pricilla and said, 'My mother never lived to see me married. But it was not all bad because I was able to meet Jesus and travel with him and his followers. And although certainly not planned, I have been able to make this great journey.'

I am not sure what Cecilia thought of my answer, but Pricilla and Aquila understood and agreed my mission is important. We continued our conversation late into the evening.

In Rome Pricilla introduced us to numerous friends and found a place for us to stay. The Aurelia s' son and daughter had just been married, freeing up a room. They needed a third bed, but Salome volunteered to sleep on a mat on the floor, explaining that the three of us often slept on the ground or in very crude inns while following Jesus. Salome assured them that just having a place in a house was a blessing.

We enjoyed our visit with Aurelia, Pricilla and Aquila and our opportunities to explore Rome. However, our stay lasted longer than planned because an early winter storm delayed us. Once again we had time to meet with many people and spread the message of Jesus and the Way. We felt we convinced many people to repent and follow the teachings of Jesus. This made up for our disappointment in Ephesus.

As I traveled farther into the Roman world, I appreciated all the more my parents hiring teachers to instruct me in Latin and Greek. I would not have gone very far without knowing these languages. As I traveled and communicated with locals, I expanded my vocabulary and became much more confident, but it was the start my parents provided that allowed this education to take place.

The young army captain we met on the ship to Rome had found spaces for us on a larger ship to Massilia. The ship carried goods for the army and was larger and more stable than the ships we had sailed on earlier. In addition to sails, the ship was powered by rows of sailors with oars on each side of the ship. In this way the ship maintained a good speed even when there was little wind.

The weather finally improved. The rain ceased, skies cleared, and the strong winds calmed. The captain of our ship to Massilia sent word he was ready to sail. We said our farewells to Priscilla and Aquila and prepared to leave for the final part of our journey west. We had enjoyed our stay but were anxious to continue on.

When we boarded to ship the captain apologized for the delay, but we assured him we understood and were glad he had not attempted to sail in such bad weather. He said he had heard about our previous passages and hoped we would bring him such favorable weather. I said that God had aided us so far and I was certain he would continue to do so. I didn't tell him of the burial cloth of Jesus, still secure in my bundle, that I considered a talisman.

Thanks to our Roman friend, the captain knew of our mission and was curious himself. As we shared our story with him during the trip he was very interested, asked many questions and, at the end, was ready to jump overboard and be baptized."

After relating this long account, Maria paused and took a deep breath. Marcus stood, stretched and said, "That was an impressive and bold undertaking. God must have been looking out for the three of you for you to have made it safely here." Marcus sensed Maria had more to say so he retook his seat.

Maria began again, "Our journey westward was one of many steps. Greek and Roman ships stopped at many points, and we often had to locate another ship sailing west. It took several different ships and many months, but we eventually reached Massilia. Perhaps God was watching over us as we found good ships, good weather and good sailing.

"Naturally, as we traveled, we told our stories of Jesus, our travels with him in Galilee and his message of the coming of the kingdom of God. Our message of 'repent and sin no more' was often not received well by the sailors. It was like sowing seeds on bare rock, but we hoped some would fall into a crack filled with fertile soil where they would grow and flourish.

"Our journey here was something of a miracle. We not only had good weather and smooth sailing, but we were also able to find ships that would take us westward. That was not always easy. Many sailors feared that having a woman on board would bring bad fortune, such as storms and shipwreck. They believed that having three women on board would certainly invite disaster. However, because we always had such good sailing, we were viewed as good omens.

I think some people believed we were witches but at least they saw us as good witches. Word spread and we were accepted on enough ships that we eventually arrived on the coast near Massilia.

Our journey was not without a few problems, however. As I mentioned, when we reached Rome, a great storm also reached the city. Rather than simply staying in our hosts' homes, helping with cooking and household duties, we began talking with people in the neighborhood. Within weeks we were well-known in the market place and piazzas as followers of the Way.

What had appeared to be a problem, our delay in Rome allowed us to speak with many people about the coming of the final judgment, the coming of the kingdom of God and the need to repent. Our message of salvation through faith in Jesus won many converts. No doubt the delay was part of God's plan."

Marcus was impressed that Maria and her companions had so few problems on their long journey from Israel to Gaul. He knew of the dangers of ship travel because he had made trips by sea and talked with many merchants and sailors. He knew of the terrifying storms and ship wrecks, delays and unpleasant crews. Yet Maria and her friends seemed to always have had good weather, calm seas and favorable winds. Surely God had favored them on the long trip.

Maria was very modest. She talked about her travel to Gaul as if it had been just a short voyage. She omitted many of the hardships and difficulties she and her two friends endured. But Marcus knew the dangers, the difficulties of simply finding a ship going in the right direction, a ship with space for travelers, a captain willing to take passengers, especially three women.

She had to have the ability, the confidence to deal with hesitant and unreasonable captains, rough crews and unscrupulous merchants. Clearly, she had these talents and abilities; she was not some simple rural maiden.

Maria had to be strong and resourceful, willing to sail for days on a ship with only a cramped space between cargo in the dark below deck. She had to be able to sleep on a hard surface with only a blanket for comfort. But, Marcus recalled, she often did that while following Jesus on his travels.

She had to be intelligent and knowledgeable; know something about geography and have an idea of where she was and where she wanted to go. She had to be alert and aware at all times. She obviously was a woman with those qualities.

Maria did all these things casually, she never boasted, and hardly mentioned her many challenges. A casual observer, seeing her in a market, or talking with other women, would never know about her amazing qualities. One had to sit with her and have long conversations to sense her true nature. Even then it required paying close attention to realize her true character.

After a pause, Maria continued, "Because Massilia is a large port city, it was not safe for three single women to remain there. We found a local boatman who took us across the bay to a remote area. We settled in a small city there, called Oppidum-Râ.[5]

After we had been there for a while and had been welcomed warmly by the local people, we began talking about Jesus with some of those people we saw most often. As we won converts, we grew more comfortable sharing our stories and the promise of forgiveness and salvation. Gradually we moved farther from Oppidum-Râ.

We moved eastward, staying well inland, avoiding the rougher element along the coast and the more established pagan worship in Roman controlled areas. People in the rural areas were friendlier and more open to our message. They were curious about our different appearance and speech, so that provided an easy way to begin a conversation. We continued to travel and eventually arrived in this region, staying in Tegulata.

After several years there, I began to tire. Talking to large groups became difficult. I hated to end my mission, but it became too much for me. A few years

---

[5] Oppidum-Râ was later renamed 'Les Saintes-Maries-de-la-Mer' in their honor. The people had somehow confused the name 'Salome' with 'Maria' thinking all three women were named Maria.

ago, I came to this cave. It is close enough to the town that people can still come to me. They come both to hear my stories and to bring me food and other things I might need. It has been a good solution for me. I have still been able to bring people to the Way.

I was also satisfied knowing many others in this region were now spreading the good news of the Way. People like our friend Jeanne converted many so I knew my work would be continued and the message spread even without me speaking to potential converts."

Maria had been sitting on the edge of her stone seat and, when she finished her account of her journey, she leaned back against the stone wall and relaxed. Marcus, also sitting on the edge of his rock, was lost in deep thought, reflecting on what Maria had told him.

He sat quietly for a while before saying, "What a story. What an adventure. Great good has come from what was almost a tragedy." He again fell silent.

After a while Marcus stood, walked over to Maria and took her hands in his. He said quietly, "Thank you so much for sharing your incredible story. I will remember it always and share it with others. People should know what you risked to bring the words of Jesus to this remote area."

As was their custom, they ended their visit with a brief prayer of thanks and hope for the future. Marcus squeezed Maria's hands and turned to leave, saying he would soon return to visit with her again. Before he could go far, she called out to him.

Maria had a serious expression and said, "Yes, please return soon, just to visit. Would you also tell Jeanne to come to see me? I have been here many years and I am growing old and have a special gift for Jeanne. There is something I have never told anyone, even my close friend Jeanne. It is important that you bring her with you on your next visit."

Marcus, of course, was eager to please Maria and said, "I will bring her as soon as she is able to come."

During the several years that Marcus had known Jeanne and her family, they had become good friends. One reason was their mutual devotion to the teachings of Jesus and also the fellowship of the tight knit community of followers. Jeanne had converted Marcus to the Way early in their friendship and Marcus was very grateful for that.

Jeanne was of moderate height and a bit stocky. She had brown eyes and auburn hair, usually bound up with a strip of cloth. She was a serious woman but had a pleasant demeanor and an easy laugh. Her three children brought her much joy.

Like all women in the region, she worked hard keeping house, tending the garden, gathering firewood and helping to mind the farm animals—a few goats, cows and a horse. Although her husband, Donnadu, was a prosperous shop owner in town and served on the town council, basics of home life kept them both busy. They found happiness in their work and enjoyed their time together.

Jeanne's husband came from a long line of prosperous farmers who had, over centuries, acquired large tracts of land. The land was fertile and, at the hands of knowledgeable farmers, very productive. The family had lived for generations in a large stone house situated on the highest point of the gently rolling land.

The family had always treated neighbors with fairness and generosity. As a result, they were respected and well liked. Jeanne's husband, like his father, was a member of the town council and at times served as its leader.

When Marcus told Jeanne of Maria's request, she was eager to go. She had missed her dear friend and realized it had been many months since her last visit.

The next day, Marcus brought Jeanne with him. It had been a long time since Maria and Jeanne had seen each other. They embraced warmly as close friends following a long absence. Maria asked Jeanne about her husband, her children and her parents. They conversed for some time about Jeanne's family, her husband's position within the leadership of the region, his travels and growing wealth and influence. They also talked about old friends, new converts to the Way and news from the east.

Then it was time for Maria to share the untold part of her story.

Chapter Eleven

The Crucifixion and Conclusion

Maria delayed telling Jeanne and Marcus certain details about the crucifixion because the memories were still so painful. So far she had only told each of them the minimum. She still wanted only to share the complete story with her closest friends. Now Maria felt the time had come. Her choice was easy because Jeanne and Marcus had both become very close to her. Even so it had taken until now to reach this point. In her many conversations with Marcus, she had now covered the teachings of Jesus and her own life story. Because the crucifixion was such a significant part of the story of Jesus and the plan of salvation, Maria felt she must tell the full story and now was the time to do so.

 Once Jeanne and Marcus had taken their seats on a ledge near the fire just inside the cave, Maria said quietly, "There is one part of my story I have never told anyone, not even you who have become so dear to me. It has simply been too difficult for me to think about it. But now it must be told.

Earlier, when I told you of the crucifixion of Jesus, his resurrection and my involvement, I gave only a brief version. Now I must give you some important details. There are things you will need to know when I am no longer here.

When Jesus decided to celebrate Passover in Jerusalem, we were all excited. Some of us hoped this celebration would be the time when the Jews would revolt and drive the Romans out of the holy city. We slept little that night, anxious for the next day's actions."

Maria hesitated as strong emotions swept over her. The memories of that time, of those tremendous events, were overwhelming. It took a moment for her to compose herself. Finally she continued, "Events the next day did not go well. The large crowds that had welcomed Jesus when he entered the city the previous day did not reappear. Small groups gathered at various places in the city, but not near the temple. No one was certain what would happen. Friends brought rumors and I stayed with a few friends at a home just outside the city."

Maria, clearly affected by the memory of the events she was describing, again had difficulty proceeding. After a pause she began again.

"It all happened so fast. On his entry into Jerusalem the first day, Jesus was met by cheering crowds. It seemed as though he was about to lead the Jews to overthrow the Romans. But, by the next day, the Jewish leaders came down on the side of the Romans. They thought that any revolt would fail, and the Romans would punish all Jews, whether they participated in the revolt or not.

"We were caught off guard by what happened next. It was as if everything we had wanted, had expected, had been turned upside down.

It was afternoon when one of the disciples came to the house where I was staying. He said the Jewish leaders had forced the Romans to convict Jesus of treason and sentence him to death. He would be crucified soon, that very afternoon. He said the disciples feared for their lives and would stay in hiding, remaining in the home of a friend.

A few other followers and I — my friends Maria and Salome and several other women — went to the field where crucifixions were held. We saw Jesus and two other men brought to the field by Roman soldiers. Jesus was forced to carry part of the cross, a heavy beam he could barely support. He was covered in blood, sweat and dirt. He clearly had been beaten and scourged. We could hardly bear to look at him. The Romans have a way of making pain and suffering visible.

The Roman soldiers nailed the men to the timbers and lifted the crosses upright. We could see the pain in Jesus' face as he tightly closed his eyes when he was lifted up. The sky suddenly grew dark, and a strong wind blew dust high into the air. The quickness and ferocity of the wind caused many people to leave in a hurry.

"I stood with Jesus' mother and the other women as Jesus cried out and finally, after lingering in pain a long while, died."

Maria again found it difficult to continue. The horrors of that day overwhelmed her, and she struggled to finish her account of the horrific events.

Maria finally continued, "As the sun was about to set, the other women and I began to worry about the body of Jesus still hanging on the cross. Jewish law said the dead must be buried quickly, but, of course, the Romans had no such concerns. Their tradition was to leave the bodies on the cross or throw them into a pit and cover them with lime. We could only wait and watch."

Once again Maria was overwhelmed with emotion. She shifted uneasily on her seat and looked at the ground before looking back at Jeanne and Marcus and said, "Salome and I watched from a distance as two men took the body of Jesus from the cross. We didn't recognize the men at first but the one giving directions looked familiar. As Salome and I talked, we remembered seeing the man before.

To go back a bit, the women following Jesus sometimes sat on the edge of the crowds, avoiding the mass of unpleasant smelling men. Two or three times I noticed a man, better dressed than ordinary villagers, standing alone at the edge of the crowd. The men near me recognized him as a member of the Sanhedrin and thought it strange that he would come to hear Jesus. They thought perhaps he was a spy for the Jewish leaders.

Later the man, named Joseph, told me he was a believer but could not speak up to defend Jesus because of his position and he was not there when the council voted to condemn Jesus. Joseph said that because of Jesus' righteousness and his unjust murder, he felt he had to save the body from the common pit the Romans used for executed criminals. It was also his duty as a Jew to see that Jesus was buried before sunset.

Joseph said he identified himself to the guards and reminded them that Pontius Pilate had not condemned Jesus. He had, in fact, washed his hands of the affair right in front of the mob. After some discussion, the guards allowed Joseph to have the body.

My friends and I followed the small group to the tomb Joseph had arranged for the burial of Jesus. Joseph saw us there and told us to return after the Sabbath to anoint the body. He said it was too late in the day to buy the necessary oils or even to wash the body. We returned home, glad that Jesus at least had a secure tomb.

The next day, some of the disciples and a few others who followed Jesus secretly gathered in homes of friends. No one knew what would happen next, but we all feared the worst. We prayed that God would protect us and send us a sign."

Maria hesitated before continuing.

"On the third day following the crucifixion, my friend Maria and I set out in the early morning for the tomb. Dawn was just breaking, and the early spring morning was cool and pleasant. It was the day after the Sabbath and our first opportunity to anoint Jesus' body with fragrant oils and ointments."

Maria paused and took a deep breath. Her mind drifted back to that place and time, now so far away. However, the images were still fresh in her mind, haunting and fearful.

The two women picked their way along the rough, narrow trail, careful to step over loose rocks. They walked as quickly as they could, all the while looking for familiar points along the trail.

The white robes of the women contrasted with their dark skin and darker hair. They wore an extra shawl against the early morning chill.

The valley was, like much of the region, dry and largely barren. But now, in the early spring, low-growing wildflowers bloomed abundantly. The bright reds and yellows contrasted with the dull, dusty green leaves among the light gray and tan rocks.

The rocky walls of the valley were honeycombed with tombs. Most tombs consisted of several small, interconnected rooms excavated into the limestone.

The tombs were closed with large round stones, resembling mill stones, rolled in front of the entrances.

The trail, one of many interconnected paths, wound through the valley just outside the city walls. Even in the light of day, it was a little scary, but in the early morning light, with the long shadows, it was even more so.

Just three days earlier, a few women had watched their dear friend Jesus crucified and then laid to rest in one of these tombs. The two Marias and Salome had watched Jesus die. Only his Mother and a few other women had joined them. The many male followers of Jesus, including his remaining eleven disciples, were conspicuous by their absence. Now it was time to find the tomb and prepare the body for burial.

Finally Maria's mind returned to the present and she continued, "As we walked we discussed whether we would be able to roll the large stone at the entrance aside by ourselves or would we be able to find other mourners who could help us.

"At last we reached the tomb we sought. Or at least we thought we were at the right place. However, the tomb was open, the large stone already rolled aside. Because the tomb was not a tomb of a family we knew, but that of a stranger, we were not familiar with that part of the valley.

When we saw the open tomb we stopped abruptly and I asked, 'Could we have taken a wrong turn? Is this not the tomb where they placed the body of Jesus three days ago?'

My companion reassured me, 'No, Maria, I am certain this is the correct place, the same tomb. I clearly recall the old, bent tree just to the left of the entrance.'

As we stood there we were suddenly aware of a man standing nearby. He asked what we were doing there, who were we seeking? Startled by his sudden appearance, I could only reply with a halting explanation. The man simply said, 'As he promised, he is not here. Look for yourselves. Then go and tell his disciples.'

We did as he said and looked into the tomb, saw that it was indeed empty, and turned to leave. The man who spoke to us minutes before was nowhere to be seen. My friend and I rushed off to find some of the disciples.

At the edge of the city we encountered Peter and told him the news. Peter said to another disciple standing nearby, 'These are just two excited, emotional women. They no doubt took a wrong path and found a tomb that resembles the tomb where Jesus was placed. They all look much the same.' We tried to assure them it was the correct tomb, but they didn't believe us.

Clearly Peter was not interested in going with us, but the other disciple said, 'Remember, Jesus said he would be raised on the third day. We should at least go and see for ourselves.'

After some more persuading, Peter, still unconvinced and unenthusiastic, consented. He said to his companion, 'I'll race you,' and took off at a slow jog along the rocky path."

Several minutes later they arrived at the tomb; the other disciple just ahead of Peter, both slightly out of breath. Peter said, 'Well, it *is* open.' He stepped into the cool tomb and, being sweaty, felt a chill. The chill was amplified when he saw the body was not there. The burial cloth was folded and lying on the stone bench where the body had been.

Asking each other what could have happened and what it meant, the two disciples left. Incredulous, confused, uncertain what to do next, they walked rapidly back to the city.

When Peter and the other disciple had left, Maria Magdalene and the other Maria remained behind.

While the other Maria sat on a rock, weeping, Maria Magdalene again entered the empty tomb for a final look around. As she walked back toward the entrance to leave, she saw the burial cloths, folded on the stone bench where Jesus had lain. Maria picked up the shroud and head cloth, both stained with Jesus' blood and sweat, and held them to her breast. She started to lay them down but then held them close to herself again. She bundled them up, tied them with the sash and took them with her.

The Jews would have considered the shroud ritually unclean because it had touched a dead body and was stained with blood. Maria didn't care, because for her it would be a tangible reminder of Jesus, the man she had loved, followed and supported.

Maria sat motionless; her head bowed. She had many adventures and faced many dangers and had survived. She drew on the strength gained from these trials. She also held tight to her faith in God and Jesus. After several long minutes, she lifted her head and looked again at Jeanne and Marcus. They looked back at her, concerned, moved but unsure what to say. Soon Maria resumed her account.

"Of course, I knew that Jesus would always be with me in spirit, but this stained cloth would be a physical reminder of the brilliant mind, the great teacher, the inspiring speaker that I had followed for several years.

"My friend Maria started back along the path, and I stood alone. As I turned to leave, I realized a man was standing nearby. I was startled when the man spoke my name. It was Jesus. I reached out to him, but he told me not to touch him. He said he was about to ascend to heaven, and I should tell his disciples he would see them soon. I ran after Maria, told her what had happened, and we rushed off to tell this great news to the disciples.

I took the bundle of burial cloth home and placed it close to my bed and out of sight. Even though Jesus was no longer physically in the world, he would always be close in spirit and the shroud would be a physical comfort in my sorrow."

Maria finished her story with tears in her eyes. Jeanne stepped closer to Maria and sat beside her. She put her arm around Maria and held her close. They sat for a long time while Maria let her mind relive those memories.

Still looking down, Maria said softly, "It was all so shocking, so unexpected, so tragic, so sad. When I recounted these events to the disciples, not everyone believed me." She looked up and at Jeanne and then at Marcus, and continued in almost a whisper.

"Some people have asked me how could I not recognize Jesus at the tomb. You must remember that the last time I had seen Jesus, after the crucifixion, he was bruised and bloody, his back and arms ripped by the Roman whips. There was blood running down his face from the crown of thorns that punctured his scalp.

"When I saw him later at the tomb, after the resurrection, he was clean, and he was wearing a clean robe. Even if I hadn't been in shock, I might not have recognized him."

Again Maria closed her eyes, moist with tears, and lowered her head.

Finally Maria asked Marcus to come into the cave with her. She led Marcus into the cave almost beyond the light. After their eyes adjusted to the darkness, Maria pointed to a small wooden chest sitting in the shadows on a narrow ledge. She told Marcus to bring it out to where they had been sitting, He carried it out and carefully placed the chest on a flat rock and they all gathered expectantly around it.

Maria explained that she had it made by a local craftsman soon after she arrived in Gaul. She opened the box and took out a large piece of cloth and asked Marcus to hold one end of the long, narrow fabric. They unfolded the material and held it, so Jeanne and Marcus had a view of the full length and width of the cloth. On it was a faint image of what appeared to be two bodies, laid head-to-head. Jeanne and Marcus gasped, stunned by the image. Breathless, they asked in unison, "Is that Jesus?"

Maria said that this was the burial shroud of Jesus which she took from the tomb following the resurrection and explained how the shroud was placed under and over the body. The image was created when his spirit was released from his body and the burst of light and energy burned the image of his body onto the cloth.

Marcus and Jeanne wondered if they had heard correctly. It was so unbelievable, so miraculous they sat, unable to speak.

They continued to stare at the shroud, leaning closer for a better look. They could not believe this was real. Jeanne returned to her seat, saying quietly, "This is amazing."

Marcus echoed, "Yes truly amazing

Maria and Marcus then carefully refolded the shroud. Marcus was stunned; amazed that he was holding something so sacred.

Maria returned to her seat and looked at Jeanne and Marcus. Her voice soft and sad, she explained that she was growing old. "I have had a long and full life. I have tried to tell the story of Jesus and his message of repentance and salvation to as many people as possible.

I believed that Jesus would return before I died, to usher in the kingdom of God. Jesus said it would happen within my lifetime but now I am not so sure, perhaps it won't. But when I die, I will join Jesus in the kingdom of God to wait with him for the time the Father has ordained.

In the meantime, Jeanne, you must protect this treasure. It is the burial cloth our Lord was laid in. It will, in turn, protect you and your family. I am certain I can trust this to you. You and your family are dedicated followers of Jesus and teachers of the Way. I know your family is destined for great things. Protect this and it will protect you.

If necessary, in the future, it should be passed to another woman, it will be safer hidden among women's possessions and garments. I also believe women might treasure it more and feel a more personal, sacred attachment."

For several minutes she stood, with tears welling in her eyes. Finally, she reached out and pulled Jeanne to herself, pressing the shroud between them. After several long minutes, Maria asked Marcus to replace the folded cloth in the small box; then she held it briefly before she handed it to Jeanne.

She kissed Jeanne on the mouth and said, "As Jesus kissed me to impart his sacred truth to me, I kiss you and pass these truths to you. Continue to share the words, love and healing of Jesus with others."

Marcus continued to visit Maria occasionally, sharing news and memories. Soon however, his business required more and more time and attention. He also was required to travel more often and for longer times. Wherever he went he shared the message of Jesus and the coming kingdom of God.

After Marcus departed for what turned out to be the final time, local people continued to visit Maria several times each week. They took her food and took care of her few needs. The following spring a visitor informed Maria that Marcus and Claudine had married and were a blissful couple, bursting with affection.

The following winter Maria learned that Marcus and Claudine had a child, a bright-eyed, happy, vigorous boy. A year later, one woman, bringing food to Maria, told her that Claudine had a second child. She and Marcus now had a boy and a girl. They named the girl Maria in honor of their friend from Magdala. Visitors also told her they were all well and excited. Jeanne and her husband were very proud grandparents.

Later that winter, a villager found Maria dead, lying peacefully on the rock ledge she used as a bed. She lay on her back on several layers of cloth that cushioned her head. A woolen blanket covered her thin frame. Her face bore a slight smile as if she passed, happy to be going to meet Jesus. She rejoined the man, the teacher she had followed, greatly admired, believed in and loved. She had converted many and won many followers for him. She knew he was pleased and would welcome her warmly.

Other villagers were summoned. They carried her body into Tegulata. When she was laid to rest, hundreds of people from distant towns as well as a crowd of local people came to pay their respects.

Marcus was there of course, with Claudine and their two children. Jeanne and her husband Donnadu joined the many mourners who came to say farewell to a dear friend who had made such an impact on their lives.

They were sad to see her depart but had so many wonderful memories and knowledge of the important work that she has accomplished. Marie of Magdala had touched many lives with love, compassion, and the message of salvation.

Maria's reputation and message spread widely in France and beyond into Europe. Many churches all over the continent were named in her honor.

Epilogue

Beziers had been destroyed by the invading army. Smoke rose from the ruins and there was no sign of life. The troops had done their job thoroughly. It was clear that the defenders, few in number and poorly armed, had been no match for the well-trained and better armed invaders.

The orders from the pope were to slaughter every man, woman, and child; most of the soldiers had no problem with this horrific task. A few battle-hardened mercenaries, however, had qualms about killing women, elderly men and children. They managed to overlook a few women and children cowering under beds, in cupboards or dark, dank cellars.

When the soldiers departed and a brief, but heavy downpour had extinguished the remaining fires, a few women, children and old men emerged, frightened, dirty and alone. They gathered a few possessions and left the ruined city.

A woman named Mary and her two small children joined the exodus. Among the few clothes Mary carried was the burial cloth of Jesus, passed through generations of women to her. They walked north toward a new life.

This small band carried a love of Mary Magdalene and the teachings of Jesus she preached. The devotion to Mary Magdalene would blossom and spread over France and much of Europe during the coming centuries.

The Catholic Church, unable to restrain this devotion to Mary Magdalene, tried to use it to the church's advantage. Church leaders labeled Mary a repentant prostitute. They made her an example of one saved from serious sin. But, in so 'honoring' her, they also used her as an example of why women should not be allowed to participate fully in the church, why women should not be allowed to serve publicly in the church or be included in church leadership.

Despite these efforts, many Christians continued to revere Mary Magdalene and to promote her message as the true meaning of Christ's teachings. All across Europe, churches were named for Mary Magdalene and followers preserved her memory and teachings, 'heretical' as they were.

For centuries, the shroud was kept hidden due to persecution and wars. It continued to be passed, safely and secretly, to women in the ruling families of Gaul and, later, France.

For centuries, the shroud was passed from woman to woman, often hidden among women's clothes. It had to be kept secret because the teachings of Mary

Magdalene were considered heretical. Mary herself was still labeled a whore by the Catholic Church.

Somehow the shroud survived the persecution of Christians by Romans and others as well as the slaughter of 'heretics' by orthodox Christians. Perhaps it was the miraculous nature of the shroud that protected both the burial cloth and its owners.

Eventually, at a time of societal change, the shroud was made public. It reappeared in 1354 in Lirey, France. It was held in high regard by many of the devout and its authenticity questioned by many others. The history of the shroud, now known as the Shroud of Turin, because it is housed in the Cathedral of San Giovanni Battista in Turin, Italy, has continued to be one of inspiration, doubt, and near miraculous survival. It is a good metaphor for the tradition and message of Mary Magdalene.

APPENDIX

For those who want more information about this amazing woman.

Sources

There are eleven references to Mary Magdalene in the four New Testament Gospels. Each is short and provides little information about Mary. In all but one she is mentioned in relation to the crucifixion and resurrection of Jesus.

Mary Magdalene is also mentioned in several of the non-canonical gospels, often referred to as Gnostic gospels. These texts were written a century or more after the New Testament Gospels and differ greatly in character.

While the content of these later texts may not accurately reflect events of first half of the first century AD, they do indicate that Mary Magdalene was well-known, highly regarded and had followers as far away as Egypt into the second, third and fourth centuries.

New Testament

New Testament references to Mary Magdalene

Matthew	Mark	Luke	John
27:56, 61	15:40	8:1-3	19:25
28:1	16:1, 9	24:10	20:1, 18

Matthew 27:55–56, 61

⁵⁵ Many women were there, watching from a distance. They had followed Jesus from Galilee to care for his needs. ⁵⁶ Among them were Mary Magdalene, Mary the mother of James and Joseph,[f] and the mother of Zebedee's sons.

⁵⁹ Joseph took the body, wrapped it in a clean linen cloth, ⁶⁰ and placed it in his own new tomb that he had cut out of the rock. He rolled a big stone in front of the entrance to the tomb and went away. ⁶¹ Mary Magdalene and the other Mary were sitting there opposite the tomb.

Matthew 28:1

¹After the Sabbath, at dawn on the first day of the week, Mary Magdalene and the other Mary went to look at the tomb.

Mark 15:40

[40] Some women were watching from a distance. Among them were Mary Magdalene, Mary the mother of James the younger and of Joseph,[a] and Salome.

Mark 16:9

[9] When Jesus rose early on the first day of the week, he appeared first to Mary Magdalene, out of whom he had driven seven demons.

[The earliest manuscripts and some other ancient witnesses do not have verses 9–20.]

Luke 8:1–3

[8] After this, Jesus traveled about from one town and village to another, proclaiming the good news of the kingdom of God. The Twelve were with him, [2] and also some women who had been cured of evil spirits and diseases: Mary (called Magdalene) from whom seven demons had come out; [3] Joanna the wife of Chuza, the manager of Herod's household; Susanna; and many others. These women were helping to support them out of their own means.

Luke 24:9,10

[9] When they came back from the tomb, they told all these things to the Eleven and to all the others. [10] It was Mary Magdalene, Joanna, Mary the mother of

James, and the others with them who told this to the apostles.

John 19:25

²⁵ Near the cross of Jesus stood his mother, his mother's sister, Mary the wife of Clopas, and Mary Magdalene.

John 20:1,18

¹ Early on the first day of the week, while it was still dark, Mary Magdalene went to the tomb and saw that the stone had been removed from the entrance.

¹⁸ Mary Magdalene went to the disciples with the news: "I have seen the Lord!" And she told them that he had said these things to her.

New International Version

All of these references to Mary Magdalene are about her role in the crucifixion and resurrection of Jesus with the exception of Like 8:1–3.

Luke 8:1–3

¹After this, Jesus traveled about from one town and village to another, proclaiming the good news of the kingdom of God. The twelve were with him, ² and also some women who had been cured of evil spirits and diseases: Mary (called Magdalene) from whom

seven demons had come out; ³ Joanna the wife of Chuza, the manager of Herod's household; Susanna; and many others. These women were helping to support them out of their own means.'

New International Version

Other Sources

Religious texts from the second, third and fourth centuries.

These texts, which date to the second, third and fourth centuries, contain references to Mary Magdalene. In some she is explicitly named, in other instances the context clearly indicates the Mary referred to is Mary Magdalene.

Most of the texts have been found in Egypt but this may simply because the conditions for preservation are much better in the dry dessert regions of Egypt. A few of these texts are known from multiple copies or fragments from more than one location. In some instances a text exists in Greek and Coptic. The copies we have date to the second, third and fourth centuries but it is possible they were written earlier.

The wide range of dates and places where the manuscripts have been found testifies to the long lasting 'fame' of Mary Magdalene. She was known and revered throughout the eastern Mediterranean into at least the fourth century.

Some texts have been considered Gnostic but recent scholarship has questioned this. Some of these ancient texts reflect variations of Christianity that existed in the centuries following the death of Jesus. The exact content is less important than the fact that

Mary is referenced and, in most texts, plays a significant role in the events described.

Some of these texts consist of a dialogue between Jesus and several of his disciples. In The Gospel of Thomas the conversation is between Jesus, Simon Peter, Matthew and Mary Magdalene. In the Dialogue of the Savior, Jesus talks with Mary, Matthew and Judas. In the Sophia of Jesus it is Mary, Philip, Matthew, Thomas and Bartholomew.

Despite the different participants involved, Mary Magdalene is the common presence. She frequently is a major speaker, often asking key questions. Clearly Mary Magdalene was among the best known of the followers of Jesus in the eastern Mediterranean during the second and third centuries.

Like modern historical fiction, ancient authors used well-known historical figures to make stories sound realistic and to add authority. In these ancient texts, names appearing often included Jesus, Peter, Andrew, Matthew, Levi, Judas and Mary. In each case, the name was a common name in the region, but people immediately knew who was meant. Jesus was *the* Jesus; Peter, Andrew, Matthew, Levi and Judas were his disciples and Mary was Mary Magdalene.

References to Mary Magdalene in other ancient texts

Sophia of Jesus Christ	Dates to AD 200s (Third century).
Dialogue of the Savior	Final redaction dates to around 150 AD.
First apocalypse of James	Estimated range of dating: 180–250 AD.
Epistula Apostolorum	Dates to the second century.
Pistis Sophia	Possibly written between the third and fourth centuries AD.
Gospel of Philip	Dated to around the third century AD.
Acts of Philip	Fourth century
The great questions of Mary Magdalene	Range of dates AD 150 to 350.
Gospel of Thomas	Scholars have proposed dates as early as AD 60 and as late as AD 140.
Gospel of Peter	First half of the second century.
Gospel of Mary	Second century.
Psalms of Heracleides	Written about AD 400.
Apostolic church order	Fourth century.

Secret Gospel of Mark   Authenticity disputed.

This list of texts is from various sources

Examples

The Gospel of Mary

One of the more obvious if not most important non-canonical source is the Gospel of Mary. This text, written in the second century, is missing many pages. What survives relates Mary's interactions with several of Jesus' disciples soon after he has left them following the resurrection.

In one scene, she comforts and encourages the disciple after the crucifixion.

Chapter 5

1) But they were grieved. They wept greatly, saying, How shall we go to the Gentiles and preach the gospel of the kingdom of the Son of Man? If they did not spare Him, how will they spare us?

2) Then Mary stood up, greeted them all, and said to her brethren, Do not weep and do not grieve nor be irresolute, for His grace will be entirely with you and will protect you.

3) But rather, let us praise His greatness, for He has prepared us and made us into Men.

4) When Mary said this, she turned their hearts to the Good, and they began to discuss the words of the Savior.

In another pertinent scene, Peter attacks Mary. Among other charges, Peter accuses Mary of receiving 'secrets' from Jesus and expresses his displeasure with Jesus' apparent affection for Mary.

Chapter 9

1) When Mary had said this, she fell silent, since it was to this point that the Savior had spoken with her.
2) But Andrew answered and said to the brethren, 'Say what you wish to say about what she has said. I at least do not believe that the Savior said this. For certainly these teachings are strange ideas.'
3) Peter answered and spoke concerning these same things.
4) He questioned them about the Savior: Did He really speak privately with a woman and not openly to us? Are we to turn about and all listen to her? Did He prefer her to us?
5) Then Mary wept and said to Peter, My brother Peter, what do you think? Do you think that I have thought this up myself in my heart, or that I am lying about the Savior?

6) Levi answered and said to Peter, Peter you have always been hot tempered.

7) Now I see you contending against the woman like the adversaries.

8) But if the Savior made her worthy, who are you indeed to reject her? Surely the Savior knows her very well.

9) That is why He loved her more than us. Rather let us be ashamed and put on the perfect Man, and separate as He commanded us and preach the gospel, not laying down any other rule or other law beyond what the Savior said.

10) And when they heard this, they began to go forth to proclaim and to preach.

http://gnosis.org/library/marygosp.htm

This tension between Mary Magdalene and Peter is common to several ancient texts and probably reflects their actual relationship during and after Jesus' ministry.

The Sophia of Jesus Christ

The Sophia of Jesus Christ is a Gnostic text. In it the savior answers a series of questions. Mary was one of several persons who asked Jesus questions. Also part of the dialogue were Philip, Matthew, Thomas and Bartholomew.

The Dialogue of the Savior

The Dialogue of the Savior is similar to the Sophia of Jesus. Those asking questions include Mary, Matthew and Judas.

The Gospel of Thomas

Gospel of Thomas contains the secret teachings of Jesus in which he makes numerous statements to his disciples. At one point three people ask questions: Simon Peter, Matthew and Mary.

Psalms of Heracleides

Psalms of Heracleides is a brief retelling of Mary's encounter with Jesus at the tomb. In it, Jesus tells Mary to reassure a distressed Peter. He also encourages her to spread his word to 'the sheep'. This parallels part of the Gospel of Mary.

Pistis Sophia

The Pistis Sophia is another ancient text with numerous references to Mary Magdalene. The text consists of a long series of questions posed to Jesus by a series of interlocutors. Mary Magdalene is prominent as the chief questioner, asking no less than thirty-nine of the forty-two questions being posed.

An example from Pistis Sophia Chapter eighty-eight — It came to pass then, when Jesus had finished speaking these words unto his disciples, that Mary Magdalene came forward and said unto Jesus: "My Lord, be not wroth with me if I question thee, because I trouble repeatedly. Now, therefore, my Lord, be not wroth with me if I question thee concerning all with precision and certainty. For my brethren will herald it among the race of men, so that they may hear and repent and be saved from the violent judgments of the evil rulers and go to the Height and inherit the Light-kingdom; because, my Lord, we are compassionate not only towards ourselves, but compassionate towards the whole race of men, so that they may be saved from all the violent judgments. Now, therefore, my Lord, on this account we question concerning all with certainty; for my brethren herald it to the whole race of men, in order that they may escape the violent rulers of the darkness and be saved out of the hands of the violent receivers of the outer-most darkness."

It came to pass, when Jesus had heard Mary say these words, that the Savior answered in great compassion towards her and said unto her: "Question concerning what thou desirest to question, and I will reveal it unto thee with precision and certainty and without similitude."

Translated by G. S. R. Mead.

http://gnosis.org/library/pistis-sophia/ps093.htm

Origen's *'Contra Celsum'* ('Against Celsus')

In his *'Contra Celsum'* ('Against Celsus') Origen of Alexandria (c. 184 – c. 253), wrote that Mary had followers. It is generally assumed that he meant Mary Magdalene. She is seen as the only Mary who might have had numerous followers at that time. She was listed along with Marcion and Marcellina, both of whom were important Gnostic leaders with many followers. Origen clearly meant Mary also had many followers and not just a few hundred in Galilee.

Note: Origen did not include any reference to Mary spreading heresies because she was simply carrying the apocalyptic message of Jesus.

Of all the groups mentioned by Origen, only Mary Magdalene is included in the several non-canonical texts described here. Clearly, Mary Magdalene was the best, most widely known and most important. If there had been a different Mary, surely someone would have identified her more fully, as was Mary of Bethany in the New Testament (John 11:1–2).

Conclusion: Mary Magdalene played a significant role in the development and spread of Christianity in the decades following the resurrection of Jesus. She deserves to have her story returned to the history of the Christian church.

Mary Magdalene possibly mentioned in Romans 16:6

An interesting but overlooked detail in the spread of the Christian message is found in Paul's letter to the Romans. In Romans 16, Paul urges the followers of Jesus in Rome to 'greet' a long list of people. One of the people listed is 'Mary, who has labored hard among you.' (Romans 16:6). The name Mary, in its various forms, is a common Eastern Mediterranean name but not a 'Roman' name. Could it be that this Mary was Mary Magdalene?